Lesser Cryptids of Greater Appalachia

A folk horror anthology

Edited by

Dawn Hilbert and Michael Fitzgerald

INTRODUCTION

Some of the creatures in these pages are nameless, others never before seen. The encounters range from the eerie to the truly weird, and the stories run the gamut from darkly comic to hair-raising. The challenging, remote terrain of Appalachia makes the existence of cryptid species not just possible, but a near certainty. The encounters themselves reflect our uneasy relationship with the rest of the animal world. Read on and be relieved that it was someone else—and not you—who experienced these strange events.

Thanks to all our enthusiastic contributors who sat with the mysteries of the still-wild places in Appalachia and then shared their visions.

Be careful in the hills!

Editors

CONTENTS

MCDOWELL COUNTY CROLE

By Rebecka Jarrell

MARIGOLD'S CHILDHOOD HOME sat disheveled, like a wet cardboard box that was slowly caving in on itself. The lawn, littered with happy gnomes, praying angel statues, and plastic flowers to replace the ones long dead, showed signs of a cursory mow at the beginning of the summer, but then had been left to its own devices.

To the untrained eye, the home only seemed in need of a good washing and some upkeep. But Marigold's eyes were drawn to the details.

Behind tattered curtains, boxes and junk peeked through the windows of both floors. Random objects had been carefully stacked on the porch and tucked behind the railings. To the left of the home sat a huge dumpster with nothing inside except Marigold's hopes about how today would unfold. The biggest sign of disarray was the one tacked to the front door:

City of Welch, WV
Unsafe Structure Notice
It is unlawful to enter after July 11th, 2004

The humid July heat beat against the rusting garbage container and uncut grass to create a hot and metallic patina that coated her tongue and

1

lodged in her throat. She lifted a hand to her nose and quickly shoved it back down into her pocket.

"Well, I'll be, if it isn't Miss Goldie Mae." A woman with slicked-back gray hair leaned on the banister of the home next door. Her tanned skin sagged and stretched over old bones and sinew as she drew a puff from a short cigarette. The first rays of sunshine were trespassing onto her porch and hit her square in the face, highlighting her glare. It was always Mrs. Danvers' highest priority to be seen as threatening, even if she was wearing lime green sweatpants and a Hello Kitty T-shirt.

"Good morning, Mrs. Danvers. It's good to see you."

Mrs. Danvers laughed and then coughed. Marigold waited. Every second here was one where she wasn't inside.

"I thought you'd become one of those city girls. Too good for places like this," Mrs. Danvers said. "Your mama done told us all about it. How proud she is'a you."

Geez, nice to see you too.

"I've just been a bit busy."

Mrs. Danvers looked at the notice on the door and her eyes slithered back to Marigold.

"Shoulda got here sooner."

Marigold said nothing because Mrs. Danvers was uncharacteristically right. She had nervously kept pushing back the days to make the trip home, until she could put it off no longer. Tomorrow was the deadline.

"There's been rumors around town." Marigold hated the way her body tensed at those words. *Just breathe.* "Your ma, I think she's becoming one of them croles. She don't come out. Not even ta church. And you know how she never missed a day a church in her life."

Dear lord, these people.

"That isn't very nice, Mrs. Danvers." She paused. No need to get caught up in the delusions of the locals.

"Croles aren't real." *Damn it. She couldn't help herself.*

Mrs. Danvers coughed again and then spit off the porch.

"Go to the city and start thinkin' you're city smart. They ran a crole right outta Beard's Hollar a few months ago. Nearly bit off poor Tommie's head. You 'member Tommie, Sally's boy."

Marigold could feel the beginning of a migraine knocking at her temple.

"Yes, that's very ni…"

"Anyways, I'm thinkin' your ma's becomin' one. I've seen glowing eyes in the windows. Watchin' me."

"Uh-huh."

"I hear things at night. Shuffling around, scratchin'. Your ma can't get around like she used to. Don't know how you plan on getting her outta there by tomorrow."

Your guess is as good as mine.

"Woulda thought she was dead if she didn't ring me every hour."

Like a sign from the heavens, Marigold's phone started ringing.

She held up her finger, digging into her purse for her phone.

"Hello?"

"Goldie, are you here? You better come on in, I got breakfast cookin'."

"Okay, I'm coming," she said loudly, sighing in relief as Mrs. Danvers retreated into her home.

She looked around at the decaying porch, then to her clothes and shoes. She debated putting her coach purse back into the car for safekeeping, but one look around the crumbling neighborhood had her clenching it tight to her side. The front door wasn't locked but she could feel the weight of something on the other side as she pushed to go in.

Goldie forced open the door and was smacked by a myriad of smells: rotting food and trash, dusty mold, and the sour smell of mildew on damp clothes. She gulped. All of a sudden, she was ten again, her friends on her porch as she desperately tried to keep the door closed. *"Grimy Goldie."*

"Come on in, Goldie!" her mother called from the back.

Marigold wanted to take her first step, but right past the entrance started the pile. Clothes and boxes and trash and books and furniture and God-knows-what sloped upwards and into the house.

She readjusted her purse and started to climb. Trying to stay upright and, at the same time, touch nothing, turned out to be a rather difficult task. Each step was precarious. Her foot searched desperately for foundation as she inched forward, sinking down as layers of garbage settled beneath her weight.

The top of the pile was so high she had to bend under the ceiling lights. Junk gathered on the stairs, making access to the second floor impossible. The room was like an ancient city submerged under water, with few landmarks to remind her of what lay beneath. The top of a Christmas tree or a lamp broke the surface.

It wasn't this bad before.

Marigold cleared her mind and pressed on, terrified that at any moment her feet or her arms would start to sink. Then she would slowly descend into the trash, arms thrashing until she was suffocated in her mother's "treasures."

The living room gave way to the hallway, and she was starting to slope down. She turned so that she slid on her bum with her feet in front of her to brace her fall.

She didn't notice her mother as she came to a stop in a small pathway that led to the kitchen.

"Goldie, I'm so happy to see you!" Her mother rushed forward, surprising her, arms pulling her into a tight hug. Goldie closed her eyes, enjoying the embrace for a brief moment before pulling back.

Her mother's face was startling. Smile lines turned downwards and hung by her chin. The bright blue eyes that had shined on her in childhood now sank deep under her brow and peered at her with suspicion. Hands that had once been strong, working home and garden, were now purpled and gnarled.

While her mother's frame seemed thin and fragile, her legs were thick, as if they would burst through her skin. Her left foot was tucked into a house slipper, while her right leg ended in a stump. She swayed slightly with an arm held out to help steady herself.

Marigold clenched her fists and blinked rapidly to keep back her tears. She imagined her mother crawling over piles of trash every day, struggling to just get food or go outside. Or pinned in place under piles of garbage, calling for help with no one to hear her.

Marigold's breath shaky, she rushed forward, wrapping her arms around her mother again.

"I missed ya, Mama."

"Oh." Her mother's surprised gasp turned to a chuckle as she melted into her hug.

"I missed you too, my flower." Her shaky hands patted Marigold's back and she pulled away to reveal her toothy smile.

"You must be starved, coming all this way from the big city."

Marigold rolled her eyes.

"Charleston ain't that big, Mama."

Her mother waved her off.

She turned back to the kitchen and hobbled along the counter, using it to balance as she hopped to the stove. Her mother reached into a stack of newspapers and pulled out two plates covered in dust. She patted them with her hand and then, giving them a once-over, decided to rinse them in the crowded sink.

Marigold watched with apprehension as her mother handed her a wet plate full of biscuits and gravy. She stood there, not sure where to go.

Her mother waved her along and Marigold turned to look at the dining nook. On one side was a recliner, covered in blankets with trinkets and trash all around, blocking the door to her old room. On the other side were more blankets in the shape of a seat.

Marigold walked over and touched the makeshift chair, only to realize it was blankets that had been precariously arranged onto the pile.

Oh god.

She turned and sat as her mother handed her a fork and an orange coffee cup. Marigold's body hummed with tension. There was a small table to her left and she awkwardly pushed things around until she made room for her cup.

Her mother had settled into her chair and was happily eating.

Here we go.

"Mama, I'm sure you know why I came."

"To see me, of course." *Oh boy. Please. Please just be agreeable this one time.*

"No. Mama, you gotta come back with me."

"Hmmmhmm, that's nice, dear."

"The city's coming to condemn the house on Monday."

Mama slammed down her hands. Marigold jumped.

"I'd like to see them try."

Marigold tried to keep her emotions in check. *Just hit her with the facts.*

"I'm serious. I've got a great place in Charleston with an apartment out back. We can garden in the summer and get you set up real nice. It'll be great."

The last sentence came out desperate. Like Marigold was trying to convince herself.

"No."

A silence shifted uncomfortably between them.

"Okay. Well, you don't have a choice," she blurted out.

Her mother's face lowered, her features darkening.

"If they wanna mow this place down, well, they can do it with me in here."

Marigold wanted to throttle her. Then she wanted to cry.

The plate of food still sat in her lap. She took one bite and chewed slowly. She reached her hand out for her cup but found nothing. It was gone. She looked at her mother who had her eyes closed and was humming lowly as she ate.

The floor wasn't clean, but it also wasn't wet. Marigold looked around the table and even under the blankets.

"What are you doin'?"

"I had a cup right here. It's gone. Like completely gone." She couldn't make sense of it.

"I'll get you another one." Her mother got up from her chair. "Finish your food."

"I'm not hungry. Sorry, I ate some snacks on the way in." Her mother took the plate from her with a huff and Marigold stood up. She thoroughly inspected the table, her seat, the floor. Nothing.

"What the heck?"

"Stuff just goes missin' 'round here. Dontcha worry about it."

Marigold tucked her purse closer to her, not wanting to lose it to whatever weird witchcraft was happening here.

It was now time for approach number two.

"So, what do you want to take with you?" she asked.

Her mother slammed a cup on the counter.

"Enuff! I ain't goin' nowhere. This is my home and you ain't got no right tellin' me what to do with it."

Marigold threw her hands in the air, exasperated. She looked around.

The back door was blocked by a stack of books and boxes. *I just have to move a few things. There's no taking her out the front.*

"What are you doing? Put that back!" Her mother screeched as she began picking up boxes and moving them to the side.

"I'm just making a path to get out."

Her mother tried to squeeze around her to block the door, but Marigold wouldn't move. She sat the boxes down and grabbed her mother by the shoulders to steady her. Her mother's hands whipped out in a frenzy, smacking her arms and head.

As she blocked her face, Marigold stumbled back into the boxes and then felt herself falling. She landed in a heap of boxes out the back door with items stabbing painfully into her back.

"Don't touch it! Don't touch anything!"

She blinked back her tears as she picked herself up. She quickly gathered herself, happy that her bag was still on her shoulder, and turned to leave.

"Goldie!"

A sudden rage overtook her and she turned back around. Her mother was still in the doorway, unable to go outside with her bad leg. Marigold picked up a few boxes and turned. She tossed them in the dumpster with a sense of satisfaction.

She walked back and picked up the rest.

"No! Goldie, you damn brat, bring that back!"

Marigold slammed the rest in the dumpster before an overwhelming sense of guilt started to creep in.

Her mother called after her, like a forlorn kitten. Marigold clapped her hands over her ears and ran to her car.

Marigold hated that she got angry, hated that she threw her mother's things out, and hated that in a fit she had stopped for cigarettes and alcohol on the way to the motel.

But she enjoyed the summer heat and the low hum of cicadas rumbling through the valley. The sound of the creek and the swaying of the trees had her sinking into a place of contentment, allowing her to fade into a mindless lull.

She was sitting at one of the picnic tables, fidgeting with her cigarette, when a red pickup truck pulled in. The man who slipped out of it was wearing his Sunday best, which around here meant a button up and khaki pants with a belt. She watched as he pulled out a smoke and strolled right over to her.

"Got a light?"

Marigold smiled. He put the cig in his mouth and leaned in close for her. His blue eyes, the kind that had girls fawning all over him in high school, flicked to her face for a moment.

"How's it going, Tommie? Heard you had a fight with a crole," she teased.

Tommie slid in across from her. He was tall with blond hair cropped short, nothing but tanned skin and muscle from years of working in the junkyard.

"Who'd you hear that from?" he asked.

"Mrs. Danvers. Then she said my mother had become a crole." Tommie huffed at that, then shrugged.

"You here to get your ma?"

"Trying. She doesn't want to leave."

"Gonna be tough, 'specially with that bum leg she's got." Marigold nodded. "I might be around tomorrow to help, but I gotta job out in Bluefield. Won't be back late in the evening."

Marigold sat up. She could definitely use the help, and her mom could potentially be swayed by someone else being there.

"I'd really appreciate it." She paused. "Wanna have a drink with me? As thanks for helping out?"

Tommie smiled at her and she knew there'd be another thing she would hate herself for tomorrow.

She couldn't make sense of it.

The back door was blocked. All of the boxes and books stacked back exactly as they were yesterday. She walked over to the dumpster and peered in. Empty.

Marigold had taken her time this morning. Instead of rushing to her mother's, she went to the local diner for coffee and then church and then back to the diner to pick at her lunch. Finally, her anxiety had morphed from worrying about going home into worrying about not being ready when Tommie arrived, and she drove to the house.

She walked to the front and hiked over the piles of junk, scrambling quickly to the kitchen. Her mind turned over the problem, but she couldn't think of any possible way her mother could have gotten her things out.

Surely, she wouldn't have called someone.

Her mother was asleep in the recliner only a few feet away, head back and toothy mouth wide open.

Marigold studied the stack. It was exactly how it was yesterday except for one thing. At the tippy top sat an orange coffee cup. She set her purse down and plucked it from the top.

Her hand clenched the mug.

What the hell! She's messing with me!

Her anger quickly rose. Her mother had seriously called one of her neighbors and gotten them to put everything back for her.

We don't have time for this!

She wanted to just throw something. She turned and looked at the mountain of junk crowding the house. Before she knew what she was doing, she wound back her arm, desperate to throw the stupid cup as far away as possible.

Suddenly, it was ripped from her hand before she could throw it. She twirled, ready to argue with her crazy mother.

Instead, she saw a long, clawed hand holding the cup.

She blinked, shaking her head to clear her mind. A hand, like that of a rodent, with five long, hairy fingers ending in sharp nails, was sticking out of the mound of junk.

She stood mesmerized as it slowly receded into the pile.

Marigold hardly took a breath as she watched. She waited a moment, heart pumping loudly in her ears, and then slowly moved forward. The hole was folding in on itself as junk shifted and, just as it was about to close, she caught a glimpse of a glowing red eye peering out at her.

Marigold was screaming. She wasn't sure for how long, but her mother was suddenly shaking her furiously, yelling her name.

She pointed, but no words would leave her open mouth.

"I know, I know, dear. It's alright," she soothed.

Marigold turned to her mother, eyes wide, not understanding.

"There's something in there," she finally got out.

"It's okay. He ain't gonna hurt no one."

Marigold's mind was slowly catching up.

"What?"

Her mother patted her hand like she was a small child with a nightmare.

"I'm so happy you're back. I'll make breakfast." She shuffled past her to the kitchen and started pulling out silverware like there wasn't some freakish creature in her house.

Marigold was shaking her head back and forth.

"Mama, I think we need to leave. Right now."

She ignored her, of course. Marigold sensed some movement from her left and threw herself against the outer wall. All she could hear was her mother's light humming and the sound of bugs outside in the muggy, summer weather.

"Mama, please," Marigold whispered.

Her mother handed her a biscuit filled with jelly and butter. She then set another biscuit onto the hoard. Marigold watched as the hand reached back out and snatched the food. Her mother looked at her with a satisfied smile. As if to say, told you so.

"Oh my god."

Marigold tried to think through what to do next but her mind could not process what she was seeing.

Was that a crole? Croles are real? It can't be real. How? Why was it here?

"We need to go. Now." She grabbed her mother by her shoulder, tugging her toward the back door.

"No! Let go of me." Her mother's face contorted into anger as she twisted away. The hoard beside them started to shake and quiver.

"Mama, please. You can't stay here," Marigold begged, fear and anxiety crowding her thoughts. She reached for her mother's hand and looked her in the eyes. For a moment, she saw hesitation.

Marigold felt a fleeting moment of hope. *Yes! Let's go.*

"He's been here for me, Goldie," her mother whispered, almost a whimper. "When nobody else was." The confession punched Marigold in the gut.

She thought of every ignored phone call. Every "no, not this time" when her mother invited her to visit.

One arm burst out of the trash and then another. Behind her mother's small frame loomed a dark shape with red eyes and a massive beak. Marigold's hand tightened around her mother's and tried pulling her forward. The crole's arms wrapped around her mother and she slipped from Marigold's fingers. Her mother touched the crole's hand comfortingly and she glared at Marigold.

"Leave us! Leave us alone!"

The tower of carefully placed boxes crumbled beneath Marigold's hands, and she stumbled into the backyard. She got to her car and tried opening the locked doors. She patted her pockets.

My purse. It's inside.

She looked back. Through the window, she could see the dark shape of the crole, watching.

She ran to Mrs. Danvers and banged on her door, but she had already left for evening service. No cars passed by in the time she waited. Most people were winding down from church and getting ready to settle into the new week. She couldn't call anyone, since her phone was still in her purse.

The world was growing dim as the sun began to set and mountains cast their shadows across the valley.

She just needed to wait for Tommie. He would help.

God, how do I even explain to him?

Marigold shivered. She did not want to be outside in the dark. The sun was setting, and she needed to decide what to do.

Her mind turned back to her mother, her face. The greedy eyes of the crole as it looked at them. Her mother's fear in that one moment of clarity.

"Mama!"

Marigold hovered in the back doorway. She looked down the hallway over the mound of trash. Nothing.

"Mama! Where are you?"

Between the kitchen and the dining nook, there was nowhere that her mother could be hiding. Marigold slowly followed the wall, ready to bolt out the back door at any point.

Her mother's musty, old chair was covered in layers of blankets, and behind it, the door to her room now gaped open.

Her breathing quickened.

She inched forward, every crunch and creak jolting through her body.

On the ground, where the door was ajar and pushed back against the piles of trash covering the bedroom, lay her mother's glasses. She picked them up and clenched them gently before setting them on the chair. She took a deep breath and entered.

Her childhood clothes, CDs, and books were strewn across the room in small hills and valleys. No, not valleys. Holes. Passageways burrowed into the floor, in the walls, even one in the ceiling.

The center of the room sloped upwards like a volcano rising out of the floor. She inched forward until she was at the top, looking down into a deep pit. A cool breeze feathered her face as her eyes adjusted to the darkness.

She was on all fours now, leaning over and looking. She could see the bottom, only about 15 feet below. In the darkness, a pink flower slipper shined like a gem.

Nope. I can't do this.

She started to slink back but the ground underneath her crumbled. The feeling of being weightless filled her with fear as she desperately swung her arms for balance. Before she could get out of the way, she was sliding forward and into the dark.

She hit the ground hard.

"Ow!"

She lay for a second, trash slowly streaming down around her and then coming to a stop. She blinked up tearily and breathed the moist air.

Hurriedly, she got up. The moment her weight settled on her right knee, she buckled in pain. She reached up and tried pulling herself up with her arms. The surface of the wall crumbled under her fingers.

No.

She rolled slowly and stood on one leg. The mouth of the hole loomed above her, about three times her height. She desperately leaned on the wall and tried pulling herself up again, but dirt and garbage just floated down on her head.

Her lips quivered and she coughed.

The passageway went further but Marigold kept her back to it as she huddled against the wall. Shivers racked her body as the cold air seemed to creep into her clothes and then her skin. She couldn't go up but she didn't want to go down.

She didn't think. Dared not to think about anything. She just moved, hobbling along the wall. Her eyes adjusted to the darkness and, as she moved along the tunnel, a dim light glowed from around a corner.

Then, there she was. Her mother was tucked into a pile of trash, a halo of flowers surrounding her head. Her cast iron pan held in her left hand with her bible tucked under her arm. Her right hand reached out to her side, palm down as if she were a puppet tied by strings.

"Mama," it was barely a whisper.

Marigold stumbled forward, pain forgotten, her hands reaching for her mother's face. Cold. Ice cold.

"No," it came out as a sob. "No, please, wake up."

She was touching her hair, her sunken face. Her pale skin was bruised and purple around her neck and near her eyes.

In life, her mother had looked gaunt, but in death, her face had softened. A small smile tugged at her lips.

"No, no, no." Marigold was shaking now.

She cried and slammed her hands down until no tears were left. Then she would look at her mother and start all over. As reality sank in, her mind spun for what to do.

I have to call 911.

She turned and, instead of seeing the light from the tunnel entrance, realized it was blocked by a dark shape.

Marigold leaned back as it stepped forward.

It towered over her, its beak clicking. She could see it clearly now. It was large but squat like a chubby mole with fur and feathers.

Its long, clawed hands reached out and pushed her to the side. She fell and pain radiated up her right leg. Her knee was on fire.

The crole tidied the area around her mother, touching the flowers, situating her hair. The glasses and slipper she had passed earlier were pulled from a pouch at its stomach. It lovingly tucked the slipper on her swollen foot and placed her reading glasses beside her.

Marigold watched in horror and interest. It was unlike anything she had ever seen. The crole was gentle, like a mother tending to her child.

More and more things were pulled from the pouch. An old pen, a worn coffee cup, a pair of knitting needles. All the things her mother had loved. Although Marigold was sure her mother would have claimed to have loved every piece of junk in this house.

Marigold started to inch backwards, back down the tunnel.

It looked at her and rose to its full height. It reached into its pouch and produced her purse. Marigold looked at it and then looked at the crole.

"Oh," she tried for politeness, "thank you."

It carefully pushed aside one of the blankets on her mother's right side to reveal another seat.

It tucked her purse into the side and turned to look at her expectantly. A chill crawled up Marigold's fingers through the ground. Her vision blurred as her heart beat loudly in her ears.

"It's okay," she whispered. "I don't need it."

Its long hands wrapped around her legs and dragged her forward. The pain was unbearable and she screamed.

"No no no no," she cried.

The crole's face twisted. Every moment that had seemed timid and dainty when tending her mother now seemed violent.

It forced Marigold into the spot, and she heard a crunch before feeling pain stab up her back. Tears slid down her face. It leaned over her, and she struggled to breathe. She could feel its heat, smell the dirt and fur and musk.

Its beak filled her vision as it started picking at and sniffing her hair, patting her clothes down. It put the purse strap on her shoulder and then tried to force her mother's hand into hers. The stiff arm snapped and cracked until the crole bent it to Marigold's.

It interlocked their hands then backed up to review its work. Marigold could barely register what was happening. She could only stare at the crole as it stared back at her. Her and her dead mother. It bobbed its head up and down excitedly.

Then it turned and disappeared out of the hole. Marigold tried to move. She really did. But every muscle shrieked in pain with the slightest twitch. She could only watch as the entryway filled with dirt.

"It's a damn shame," said Mrs. Danvers.

Tommie took a long puff of a cigarette and sighed. Marigold's car still sat in the driveway of the old home and he wondered if he'd have to take it to the junkyard himself.

"Yep."

"You think they'll find something?" Tommie surveyed the home as the bright police lights flashed against the siding in the darkness. He shrugged.

"It's in there, in'it?"

"It was." Mrs. Danvers glared at him.

"There weren't a trace of it left when I checked," he added, hoping that would shut her up.

The officers filed out, shaking their heads. They wouldn't find anything, but they sure as hell weren't looking that hard either. Sometimes, it was better that way.

Tommie rubbed his sore shoulder, tracing the healed indent in his skin from an oversized beak bite. His eyes strayed to the mountains.

"It'll be back. It can't help itself."

A POOL OF TEARS

A *Paranormal Appalachia* Story
By JD Byrne

VICTORIA TURNED OFF the main road onto the long gravel drive. They wound back into the woods just as the last song finished. Tall hemlocks lined the drive, branches arching out like a cathedral ceiling, allowing only occasional shafts of late afternoon sun to pierce through. "That was lucky timing."

"Good planning," Ben said, disgorging the CD from the dash and filing it away in the box he'd brought. "At least your behemoth still has a CD player."

"It's not a behemoth, Ben, it's an Outback. Just because it wasn't built in the 1960s by leprechauns . . ."

"Colin Chapman was a genius, not a leprechaun," Ben said, referencing his beloved Lotus. "Colin Farrell on the other hand . . ."

Victoria pulled the car up in front of the two-story, rough wood cabin. It had a porch running along the front, with a pair of Adirondack chairs off to one side. Around back was another porch with a big swing. She'd pulled Ben away from his investigations and the website he ran by selling a weekend unplugged and offline. The locale clearly made an impression.

Ben leaned forward. "Explain to me again how you have access to this serial killer's hideout?"

"Yvonne is a sculptor, not a serial killer," she said. "She inherited this place from some dead relative. Comes out here to disconnect, brainstorm new pieces."

"And sometimes lets you use it?"

"When I sell something of hers, yes," Victoria said, proud that she'd finally moved that round, gray monstrosity out of the gallery's display window. "Don't worry, London boy, nothing out here is going to hurt you."

Ben didn't seem convinced.

"Look, how about you unload the car," she said, handing him the keys, "and I'll handle the two monsters." She turned to examine the back seat. There, Ben's dog Billy, a ginger terrier mutt of some kind, and Klimt, her beagle, were snuggled up and entwined so tightly with each other she feared they might have achieved a singularity. If there was gay dog love, these two had it.

"Deal," Ben said, stepping out of the car.

Victoria got out and opened the back door, grabbing up the two leashes. "Come on, guys! We're here!" The enthusiasm was just barely enough to rouse them.

The dogs came to life once their paws were on the ground and the scents of the woods hit their nostrils. As usual, Klimt led the way, with Billy jogging a few steps behind. They headed around the cabin and toward the woods behind. In a few steps the lush evergreens enveloped them.

After they'd taken care of their business, Billy and Klimt returned to their nasal exploration of the area between the cabin and the tree line. Billy seemed pretty aimless, if content, but it wasn't long before Klimt picked up some particular scent that interested him.

"What ya got?" Klimt began tugging her back toward the cabin and Billy soon joined in. "All right, let's go see how Ben's making out."

The closer they got to the cabin the more eager the dogs were, although they didn't break out into barking. Above the constant snuffling Victoria heard something, or someone, up ahead.

They were crying.

She reined in the dogs, kneeling down to shush them as best she could. There was definitely crying going on around the corner. Had something gone wrong? This was her first trip away with Ben and all had been smooth, so far as she knew. It didn't really sound like Ben, but then she'd not heard him full on weeping so far in their relationship, either, thankfully.

After a moment, the crying stopped. Victoria stood and led the dogs around the corner. There was nothing there, certainly not her boyfriend having some kind of breakdown. She looked down to see a small puddle of water, of the kind you find beneath gutters that weren't doing the best job. But no Ben and nothing else, either.

"Come on, you two," she said, pulling the dogs along.

Ben was hefting the cooler out of the car when they turned the corner.

"Everything all right?" she asked.

He closed the hatch. "Aside from us bringing every item known to man for a quick weekend getaway? Yes, everything's great. Why?"

"You weren't just bawling your eyes out over there, were you?"

"No?" He pronounced it slowly like he wasn't sure there was a right answer. "Why would I have been?"

She shook her head. "My ears must be playing tricks on me."

The cabin was elegant, as you'd expect from an artist's lair, but basic in modern terms. There was a nice TV setup, with a Blue-Ray player and collection of movies, but no cable. There was no internet connection and, given the rugged terrain, neither of their cell phones got consistent reception. Charmingly, there was a landline phone, in case of emergencies.

But Victoria had forgotten how quiet it was. There were no city sounds, even the kind of road noise and such that you had back home in

Sutton. A breeze would waft through the trees, but otherwise you could be forgiven for thinking everyone else on Earth had just disappeared.

Until the gunshots woke her up the next morning.

"The hell was that?" She sprung upright in bed as the dogs started howling in the next room.

She jumped to her feet and pulled on a pair of sweatpants and sweater. "Get the dogs," she said, rousing Ben.

Two more shots rang out.

Ben sat up and rubbed his eyes.

"I'm going to see what's going on."

"Where the gunshots are?"

"It's not a gang war, Ben. Probably just a lost hunter. Still, I'll be careful. You just corral the dogs somewhere."

Victoria walked through the living room, keeping the dogs at bay and slipping out the door. She scanned the woods from the front porch, but didn't see anyone or anything. Then another shot rang out, from near the back of the cabin. She ran down the steps and around to the back, waving her hands and shouting. "Hey! Whoever's shooting! Please stop!"

In the woods she heard a rustle of leaves. A man walked out of the woods, shotgun in one hand. He was wearing a blaze orange vest with assorted pockets and places to hold additional shells. He cracked the shotgun open, disgorging a spent shell, and draped it over his arm. "Sorry. Didn't realize anyone was here this weekend."

"Who are you?" Victoria brandished her phone like a shield, even though there was no signal out here. She thought about taking his picture.

"Morris Turner," he said, "friend of Yvonne's. This is her cabin."

She nodded. "Victoria. Also a friend of Yvonne's. She's letting me and my boyfriend use the place this weekend." She realized this was the first time she'd referred to Ben that way.

He slung the shotgun over his shoulder. "Sorry, but Yvonne told me I could hunt here anytime she wasn't around. Been here about a week, with another to go. My place is over that ridge." He gestured ahead into the woods.

"I'm sure it's lovely, but you can't just come around guns blazing."

"Hadn't seen anyone around." He stiffened. "But I'd never shoot at the cabin."

"Because we'll never have to take the dogs out or just enjoy a nice walk in these woods while you're hunting," she fired back. "Can't you understand that?"

He put up his hand. "Truth is, this isn't getting it done for me anyway, the game I'm after. But I'd like to be able to keep tracking, if it comes through this area."

Victoria didn't want to back down, but neither did she want to anger the guy with the gun. "I better go call Yvonne." She waved him to follow around front. "You do this a lot, then, do you? Hunting?"

Morris chuckled. "I usually stick to exotic game in far-flung places. I've bagged all five of the big African game animals, even a rhino. Then there was the elephant in Cambodia, kangaroos in Australia. You ever tried to bring something down that leaps like that?"

She rolled her eyes, glad that he was behind her. "Never had the pleasure. I didn't think anything was in season right now."

"Oh, there's no season for squonk," he said.

They reached the porch before she could ask what he meant. "Why don't you stay out here? I won't be a minute." She rushed inside before he could object.

Ben was leaning on the kitchen counter while the dogs scratched and sniffed loudly from the bathroom. "Get it sorted?"

"Maybe," she said, fishing Yvonne's number from her phone. "Go keep him company?"

Ben wordlessly headed out to the porch. Before the door closed she heard Ben introduce himself and Morris make the inevitable remark about Ben's accent not being from around here.

It took two tries, but Yvonne finally picked up. She confirmed what Morris had told Victoria, although she admitted she'd forgotten about it. Yvonne was deeply apologetic about the mix up, but begged Victoria not to run Morris off completely.

"He's an asshole, but he's friends with one of the most important gallery owners in the Midwest," Yvonne said. "I can't afford to piss them off. Does it really matter if he's running around in the woods while you're there?"

Victoria sighed to herself. "We'll just keep the drapes closed, I suppose."

"That's the spirit!" Yvonne said, before hanging up.

Victoria found the two guys on the porch. "Well?" Morris asked.

"Yvonne confirmed what you told me," Victoria said. "I think we can get along just fine for the weekend, as long as we can agree to a couple of things."

"I don't know, honey," Ben said, "Morris here was just regaling me with how he was able to convince an African chieftain to let him hunt on ancestral lands. Showed me some pictures of his trophies, too! He might drive a hard bargain."

Victoria ignored him. "First, don't use that thing anymore." She nodded to the shotgun. "Second, if you'd try to stay away from the area immediately around the cabin? Let us enjoy nature for a couple of days."

"Deal." Morris extended a hand. "I'll try and keep my tracking to other areas until you're gone."

"Good luck with your hunt," Victoria said.

"Y'all have a pleasant weekend." He grabbed the shotgun and headed for the woods.

Inside, Ben said, "are you crazy?"

Victoria recounted her conversation with Yvonne.

"At least he agreed to stop shooting," Ben said, putting on a pot of water for tea.

"He said it wasn't working for what he was after anyway, this squonk," she said.

Ben looked up. "What?"

"Squonk. Why?"

Ben ran out the front door.

Victoria shook her head and let the dogs out from their makeshift pen. They sniffed intently around the living room, looking for clues about a potential intruder.

Ben came back in and handed her a CD case. "See?"

It was a Genesis album called *A Trick of the Tail.* She looked up. "Phil Collins' band?"

Ben rolled his eyes. "Look at the tracks on the back."

She flipped it over. Track three was called "Squonk."

He pulled out the liner notes, flipped a couple of pages and handed the booklet to her.

There were lyrics to a song about a pathetic beast so disgusting that it was frequently crying. That allowed it to escape predators by dissolving into a pool of tears. At the bottom was a drawing of a small creature, like an oversized rat standing upright, holding a handkerchief to his dripping eye.

"You're not saying," she started.

"You're sure he said squonk?"

"Of course. It's such a weird word it jumped out at me."

Ben started pacing back and forth. "I remember reading about this online years ago." He stared at the ceiling in thought. "The squonk wasn't their creation. It came out of some folk book about western Pennsylvania. I don't remember the details."

She shook her head. "How'd a British band get . . ."

"Dunno, but I'm sure that's right."

"That's silly," she said. "Why would a grown man be out hunting something that doesn't exist?" Even as she said the word "silly," she couldn't help remembering the crying she'd heard the day before, the pool of water.

Ben coughed. "Do it for a living, darling. Some of the time, at least."

"Yeah, but that's different," she said, stepping over and wrapping her arms around him. "I say we just forget him and enjoy our weekend."

Ben kissed her. "Good excuse to put on that album, though."

Victoria sighed and headed for the shower.

A slight breeze rustled the trees. In the distance an insistent frog croaked out a call for a companion. It was almost completely dark, save for the flickering light from a lantern perched on the back porch railing and the sparks of passing fireflies. Victoria and Ben sat curled up on the porch swing, sipping wine and doing not much else, while the dogs napped on the deck. This was unplugging and she was loving it.

Occasionally there were sounds in the woods, the slow steps of animals passing through thickets of limbs and leaves or crunching dried sticks underfoot.

Ben was already snoring, and Victoria had just about nodded off, when the dogs went on alert and snapped her to attention. Klimt barked once. There was a more consistent, louder, rustling of leaves in the woods. It sounded like it was getting closer. Victoria turned in the direction and saw a bobbing white light coming through the trees. It was about the height of a flashlight in the hand of someone who was running.

She stood. "Morris!"

The light stopped. "Sorry! I got caught up," he said from the woods. "Damned thing got away again!"

"How about you call it a night?"

"Sure, sure. Didn't mean to bother."

Victoria watched the glow of the flashlight slowly fading as he walked away. "You believe that guy?"

The dogs and the yelling had finally awakened Ben. "He's very determined, I'll give him that."

The dogs were still straining at their leashes. Neither Klimt nor Billy was barking or snarling, but they each looked like they had picked up the scent of something nearby. Victoria could have sworn she heard sobbing similar to what she'd heard when they arrived. "Grab the lantern."

She let Klimt guide her off the porch, toward the tree line. Ben and Billy followed, rushing to catch up.

At the edge of the woods, between two tall hemlocks, was a tangle of bushes and brambles that was shaking back and forth. The sound of deep, heartbreaking sobs was coming from it. Klimt stepped forward, cautiously, then started pawing at some of the brush.

"Give me some light," Victoria said, kneeling down beside the dog.

Ben positioned himself so that the lantern was directly above.

She started pulling away limbs and leaves with one hand, while holding Klimt at bay with the other. Billy wandered back and forth around the other side of the bush, sniffing like mad. It didn't take long for her to realize there was something alive, some creature, caught up in the bush. When she finally saw it, she had no idea what it was.

It was small, about two feet tall, standing erect. It looked like the world's oldest man's skin had been taken off a full-grown human and draped over its small frame, the folds tucked here and there. Its skin was covered with what looked like warts or boils or something else Victoria didn't want any part of. One foot was webbed, the other had three toes. Everything glistened sickeningly. No wonder the look on its face was one of pure misery, pain, and unhappiness.

And it was crying, or at least trying to cry.

"Tell me this isn't what I think it is," Victoria said.

Ben was silent for a moment. "I mean, it sort of looks like it. But shouldn't it be dissolving into a pool of tears?"

Victoria studied the poor creature's face, so full of fear and desperation. "I think it's trying, but there's no more tears to cry. Who knows how many times it's had to run from Morris?"

Ben nodded. "These last few years I've seen things." He paused. "Things I'd never believe if I hadn't experienced them for myself. Impossible things. So I can't say this isn't a real, genuine, squonk. What do we do with it?"

Victoria took the lantern and put it on the ground, then handed him Klimt's leash. "We're going to set it free." She turned her gaze to the dry crying eyes of the creature. "Don't worry, we don't want to hurt you."

She started to pick at the branches and limbs that had wrapped themselves around the creature, but its agitation was constant and progress was slow. Behind her Ben started whistling a slow, sad tune. Whether he was just bored or was doing it with purpose, it had an effect on the squonk, which started to calm down and stay still at least enough to let Victoria work. Ben repeated the tune over and over.

It took about fifteen minutes, but Victoria managed to untangle the beast, save for one thin branch that was wrapped around one leg. Rather than try to finesse it, she simply broke the branch off. The little creature, suddenly untethered, lost its balance and fell over. Klimt barked and the creature quickly got back to its feet.

"Hush," Victoria said. She put up her hands and tried her softest, most comforting voice. "It's all right, little guy. You can go."

The beast stood still for a moment, surveying them with its big, wet eyes. It took a few halting steps backwards, then turned and started running. The dogs tried to chase after it, but Ben reined them in.

"That's our good deed for the day, then."

She shook her head. "Not so long as Morris is out here. He's here for another week."

"So?"

"So," she said, plan whirring to life in her mind, "how do you feel about doing a little work this weekend?"

Using Yvonne as a go-between, Victoria invited Morris to dinner the next night. She did what she could to turn the menu for a romantic dinner for two into something they could split three ways. Ben wasn't happy about the plan but had agreed to go along. He spent a long while on the phone with someone named Artith with whom he'd worked before.

"At least she confirmed what we thought," he said when he was done. "Until last night."

"That the squonk is a myth?" She was focusing on slicing a cucumber. "That's good, right?"

"That means that, aside from the two of us and the dogs, nobody can say for certain that the squonk is real, yes."

Something in his voice worried her. "You don't sound convinced."

He sighed. "It's just that, usually, this is the other way 'round. I'm the one poking holes in somebody's story, figuring out how they're wrong. But Morris is right, isn't he? This thing he's hunting really exists."

"Yes, but it's frightened and helpless and certainly doesn't need to be captured or whatever Morris had in mind for it." She had to ask the next question. "You agree, right?"

He thought for a moment. "I completely agree with that. I just don't like lying to this guy to pull it off. I know you probably don't think of it like this, but deep down I'm still a journalist. I trade in truth, or at least I try to. I've been burned before, so maybe I'm particularly sensitive to it."

She stood on her tiptoes, took his face in her hands, and kissed him. "I know it won't be easy for you, but doing the right thing seldom is."

He slowly started nodding his head. "That I know for sure."

Morris appeared an hour later, bottle of wine in hand.

"Think of it as a peace offering."

"I didn't think we were at war," she said, "but I appreciate the gesture."

Morris also brought stories of his life and a willingness to tell them. He'd made his money in petroleum and had stories of his travels all over the world. He retired early to pursue his passion for hunting rare game. While Ben cleared away the plates before dessert, Morris finished a story about tracking down a Tasmanian Devil, which he was finally able to corner with the help of his aboriginal guide. "It was a classic pincer movement, straight from the playbook of Alexander the Great." He hesitated, with practiced precision. "Which the devil had never read!" The punchline amused him more than her and Ben.

"I certainly don't have anything to compete with that," Victoria said, "but when it comes to rare game . . ." She turned to Ben. "Honey, did you tell Morris what you do?"

"Don't look much like a hunter," Morris said. "Is it fish? This Brit I know would go to the ends of the Earth just to catch a damned fish, take a picture, and throw it back."

Ben shook his head. "No, I'm actually a journalist, of sorts. Investigator of the paranormal." He pulled out a business card and handed it to Morris.

"No kidding?" Morris examined the card. "Like Bigfoot?"

"Always Bigfoot with you Yanks," Ben said. "I run a website, Paranormal Appalachia?" He paused for recognition that never came. "I report on all kinds of odd things and creatures." He started assembling dessert.

"That's honestly why we wanted you to come tonight," Victoria said. "It's about your . . . prey."

"The squonk?" His eyes went big. "You saw it? Around here, right? Ooh, last night I bet that's why you chased me away. Did you catch it? Where is it?"

Victoria did her best impression of a concerned smile. "No, that's just it. There is no such thing as a squonk. It doesn't exist."

Morris shook his head. "I've seen it with my own eyes."

"You think you have, but it's a myth, a story made up to amuse locals and baffle tourists."

Morris crossed his arms. "I have sources. People who know these woods, what they're talking about."

"I have sources, too," Ben said. He set down a pair of brownies topped with ice cream in front of Victoria and Morris and then got one for himself. "I used to work for the *London Journal of the Paranormal*. It's been around for a hundred years or more. They've got extensive archives on all kinds of paranormal things, cryptids and the like. I talked to my old editor yesterday, Artith, and had her do some digging in the archives."

"I should have known from the start." Morris picked up his fork. "You're here for the squonk, too. You're trying to put me off, keep me from bagging the beast first."

"No, we came here for a romantic weekend in the woods," Victoria said. "Do you see any hunting gear?"

He made a show of slowly putting the fork back down. "I'm not going to poke around, but I'm certain it's here, somewhere. You're not locals. I've been coming to these woods for years. People talk to me."

"Which people?" His choice of words – "coming to" instead of "lived" – suggested she knew the answer. "Rangers? Local zoologists?"

Morris waved that expertise away. "You want to know about local game, talk to locals, the people who live out in these woods. The ones that hang out in the bait shops and game butchery stations."

She fought off a smile. "That's kind of what I suspected." She turned to Ben. "What did Artith say, honey?"

"The squonk first appeared in 1910, in a book called *Fearsome Creatures of the Lumberwoods*. It was written as a kind of compendium of local legendary creatures, dedicated to capturing stories from lumberjacks, of creatures," here Ben made quotation marks with his fingers, "'he has originated.' It's no more accurate than a D&D *Monster Manual*."

"I mean, what have you actually seen of this beast?" Victoria asked.

Morris thought for a moment. "Well, I haven't actually *seen* it, not yet. I can hear it, I think I can smell it. I've heard it cry, I can say that."

"You've been duped, Morris," Victoria said. "I'm sorry to say."

Flustered, Morris struggled to respond for a moment. "You're saying the people around here lied to me?"

"They're bullshitting you," Ben said. "For fun."

Victoria jumped in. "I'm not trying to be mean but you're a lot. You brag. You come across as better than anybody else, not just the smartest person in any room but the bravest and the most cunning. Understand how that might rub people, even the locals, the wrong way?"

Morris' silence said she wasn't wrong.

"They sent you on a snipe hunt," Ben added. "Told you about this fantastic creature that didn't exist, had never been caught, knowing that you'd go after it and, ultimately, fail."

"It wasn't a nice trick to play," Victoria said, "but that's all it was. A trick."

Ben must have sensed Morris was wavering. "I'm sure there are plenty of very real animals in these woods you can kill, right? Forget the squonk and go bag an elk or something. That'll show those yokels."

Morris stood without finishing his dessert. He was vibrating, either with rage or embarrassment. He did finish his wine in one gulp. "You've given me a lot to think about. Perhaps, it's time to shift my focus. Thank you."

Before either of them could say anything, he was out of the cabin.

Victoria turned to Ben. "You think it worked?"

"For our blubbering friend's sake, let's hope."

The phone in the cabin rang the next morning while they were packing.

"Did something happen with Morris last night?" Yvonne asked, more curious than concerned.

"We just had dinner with him. Talked a bit about his current hunt. You know how he likes to go on."

Yvonne chuckled. "Well, I don't know what you said, but you managed to make that man sound humble, so credit for that."

"Oh?" Victoria smiled.

"Called me this morning. Apologized for the trouble he'd caused, said he was cutting his stay short. Said the two of you had spared him further foolishness. What's that about?"

"I think we just clarified some things for him. No problems, I hope."

"None at all, I just had to confirm," Yvonne said. "Otherwise, you two have a lovely time?"

"Lovely enough that we'd like to do it again some other time, maybe without the drama."

"Deal," Yvonne said. "Anybody who can charm Morris has a standing invite at my place. Safe travels."

"Thanks," Victoria said, hanging up the phone.

"Who was that?" Ben asked.

"Just Yvonne. She talked to Morris."

"And?"

"I think we're fine," she said, stretching to give him a kiss. "Thank you."

He nodded and headed to the car.

Victoria gathered the dogs and walked out to the front porch. Ben waved frantically as he tried to arrange everything in the back of the Outback. In her mind she could hear him cursing.

"C'mon," she said, stepping off the porch. The dogs followed dutifully, then sprang in front of her, sniffing for the perfect spot. After their business was done, Klimt started slowly pulling Victoria over toward the trees.

"Not now, it's time to go home." The dogs were undaunted, with Billy adding his weight. As they approached, she could see some of the lower branches ruffling. "Sit here, you two." To her great surprise, they did.

Taking a few steps forward, she lifted up one of the branches near the ground. Hiding behind it was the squonk, bouncing joyfully from one foot to the other. It wasn't crying. It was smiling, as best it could.

Victoria got down on one knee. "Hi. You be sure to keep your head down. I don't think you'll have to worry about Morris anymore, but who knows who else might come out here looking for you?"

The squonk did something like a nod, then reached out one of its slimy, lumpy paws. With great reluctance, Victoria touched it with her own hand. There was a moment where their eyes locked and then the beast backed away. It flogged its limb back and forth in a horrible approximation of a wave.

Victoria stood and waved back. "Be safe, little guy."

The squonk turned and ran into the forest.

Ben was waiting by the car, doors open. The dogs did their thing and leapt into the back seat, while Victoria went to the passenger's side.

"See anything interesting?" Ben asked as he got in.

"How about we agree to say I didn't see anything," she said, "and neither did you."

He nodded. "No website writeup for Ben, huh?"

"No," she said, then leaned over and kissed him. "But I hope we got something more meaningful."

Klimt barked, then Billy did the same. It was time to go home.

THE HELLBREAKER

By Zachary Smith

GRACE BLANKENSHIP STEPPED out of her tent flap as she heard the approaching sound of the engine. The campsite was strategic, even if the amenities were classified as 'primitive'. Pikeville lay to the west, where she had stopped for supplies, and in the hills to the east of her campsite was the Kentucky-West Virginia border. There began a wide swath of decapitated mountains that ran on through county after county. Just looking at satellite photos of it made her wince, like looking at a bloody wound. She closed the apps on her phone: the LIDAR scans, the weather forecasts, even the ones she programmed herself to communicate with her sensors. *Everything was in working order, just one more delivery.* She tucked her straight black hair behind her ears and laced up her hiking sandals. The young woman smiled as she noticed the leaves of a pawpaw tree in the canopy nearby.

From the gravel parking lot, there was a small trail that led up the hill to the campsite. Walking up the shadowed trail, a tall dark man carried duffel bags on each shoulder and two more in his fists. His blue sportscar parked behind him.

"You survived the gravel roads, huh?" Grace called out as she walked to the edge of the clearing where the trail ended at the campsite, motioning to the car.

"Couldn't leave on time. Practice ran late," The man gestured to his shirt, a WVU football logo with the name embroidered under it: Jakoby Jackson Jr.

"Well, I'm glad you made it! You're a huge help, babe!" Grace reached up and hugged him before he could set the bags down near the fire pit. She kissed his cheek.

"What's this?" Jay held up the package he had picked up. Grace had ordered a custom job online, but it saved forty-five dollars in shipping for her boyfriend to pick it up.

"Ah, yes! The pièce de résistance!" With eyes bright, she ignored the question as she tore the brown paper packaging off it, tossing the shreds into the unlit firepit.

She opened the large box and held up a bulky yellow plastic and metal box that looked like some sort of solid cage. It had two dials, an LCD screen with several nine-segment number displays, and a half-dozen cable connection inputs.

"Yeah… so, what *is* it?" Jay repeated.

"The beating heart of my data collection!" Grace was already busy powering it up, and connecting it to the two solar panels she had propped against the picnic table. "I have to do something big. It's my senior year, too, Jay. You want the NFL, and I want the Ivy League. You'll get your goal with more conference titles and school records. *This* is how I get to mine."

"Aw yeah, that's my woman. We on that 'power couple' energy," He laughed again and started stacking a fire, a microcosm of warmth and light in the great expanse around them.

"Come on, Jay, keep up! You aren't scared, are you?" Grace motioned into the undergrowth.

"Afraid? Psh! I'll wrestle a bear any day. Three-hundred pounds here, y'all!" Jay called out into the trees, flexing.

"Black bears can weigh over five hundred, and run a forty-yard dash in under three seconds. You're cooked! No chance!" Grace crossed her eyes and stuck out her tongue in a feigned death. "Good thing for us black bears aren't that aggressive."

"No other dangerous animals then? Just like, uh, snakes, I guess? Any wolves?" Jay looked around on the ground as they began walking into the trailhead, having left their campsite empty, loading all their supplies into oversized backpacks.

"Wolves haven't been around these parts in nearly a hundred years. Even the reintroduction of them back in Tennessee had failed. Big disappointment to the Appalachian ecologists in my department." Grace shook her head.

"Oh? Why? I thought bringing wolves back would, like, put everything back in balance?" Jay looked ahead as Grace led on the trail just a few feet in front of him.

"Well, the Yellowstone reintroduction project was more or less a success. They wanted to bring the ecosystem back into balance. But that environment was still compatible enough with wolves to allow them back in, stabilizing the elk population and such." Grace turned and let out a sigh.

"So, I'm guessing our area is…not compatible?" Jay looked around at the trees and moss around him.

"Not enough of the original system remains in Appalachia." Grace was walking faster now, the stress evident in her body about the topic. "That's why trying to document this place, Two-Fork Creek, is so important to do before any mining."

"And you think this new project is something big?" Jay was still trying to figure out her thesis.

"As a whole, the region's ecosystems are *very* disturbed. But there's always the chance some holler out there managed to stay unknown and untouched by sheer luck. Ours are the oldest mountains in the world after all. Even whole biomes, like some high elevation forests, are remnants of past eras, preserving Ice Age forests, like on Mount Le Conte for example. Some animal lineages are even older than the Ice Ages, though. Salamanders, for one! We are the salamander capital of the world here in Appalachia!" Grace looked back with glee, and shifted into sing-song: "Red-cheeked salamanders, yonahlossee 'snot otters', or giant hellbenders, oh my!"

"And that's gonna get you into Yale? Weird salamanders—really?" Jay laughed.

"Okay, not just salamanders. But if I can document some locally significant species, and such, well, then I can maybe get the regulators to reevaluate the mining approvals and I'll have a new research site! And, yes, *actually*, the salamanders are very significant! They are the most sensitive to changes in water quality. And to use a local expression: they are the canary in the coal mine." Grace motioned to the valley stretching out in front of them.

"And we just gotta hike in, hide your little devices all over, and get out while they send you the data you need? No problem!" Jay looked over the ridge as they stopped for a rest, seeing nothing but green covering a dark understory.

"I dunno if it's gonna be enough, Jay. Grad school is gonna take a big research proposal. I need this initial pilot study to come through with some strong original data. Anybody can theorize, but I need some empirical weight in my publication if I'm gonna get into a great program! But more than that, I really want to help give us more good reasons to care about our mountains."

"Is this why you were making all those little devices over spring break?" Jay held up a small aggregation of 3D printed plastic and soldered wires from the stuffed pack. Grace walked over and made a quick flip of a switch on the large yellow and metal box, pushed a few buttons, and pointed to the top section, which now had two tiny green LEDs lit. The small bit Jay held in his hand flashed a green light briefly.

"Say hello to the off-grid control unit here. I had to send it off for a custom welding job, but the internals, PLCs, and code are all my own." She pointed to two different systems with respective wires coming from a box labeled 'Data 5v' and 'Sat 24v'. "The dual system means the wireless network signal will only be detectable for sixty seconds per day. One for local upload, and the other to the cloud remotely."

"Detectable? By who?" Jay sat up, surprised.

"Martin Whaley." She answered with an expression to match the glum tone in her voice.

"That's oddly specific. Do we know him?"

"He is the recent inheritor of the watershed area I found through a historical map analysis. The area is called Two-Fork Creek. If I'm right, his land could be some of the oldest of old growth forests in the whole state. And he's trying to sell his mineral rights to some of the worst companies. My contact in the local regulator's office said he heard Whaley bribed the local inspector to sign off on mining operations without an EPA site visit! A full MTR permit! Avoiding ecological documentation for all the wrong reasons. Thus, my solution: a distributed, timed-burst network!"

Grace could tell by Jay's face that she needed more explanation.

"Ok, Jay, so the original model of the sensor network kept the wifi signal permanently online. And since it's technically, um, *trespassing*, a constant signal would be obvious, if one was looking," Grace blushed at the suggestion of a possible misdemeanor, but not enough to make her question the necessity of it. She had bigger goals, and besides, no self-respecting native of Boone County ever let their plans get off track because of a "No Trespassing" sign. She continued her monologue, Jay now nodding conspiratorially.

"And don't you remember what he said? 'Stay off my land, you tree-hugger?' And I'm pretty sure he muttered 'chink' under his breath to whoever he had there listening in with him on that Zoom call." Grace recounted. Being half-Asian in Boone County meant she had to grow thick skin with how casually some people unfurled their racism. But comments like that always stung, a mix of righteous anger and demoralizing exasperation swirled inside.

Jay snorted. "Yeah, I don't know why you wanna go back out here to the backwoods. We both got what it takes to get out. Why waste time with a place that won't treat you like you belong." Jay, biracial himself, knew that experience all too well, even more so than Grace, having a white mother and black father.

"That's just it, though, Jay. I have always felt at home in these mountains, regardless of some bigots. I had to establish that for myself early on, or else I'd have believed them. But Mother Nature says so, symbolically speaking. That's why I love the pawpaw fruit. Its relative, the soursop fruit, is a popular naturalized fruit in Malaysia, where my mom's from. I like to think of those two fruits as nature's way of saying 'There is always more to life than our preconceptions'. To me, that's a natural, if unexpected, connection between those two regions that are part of me, Appalachia and Southeast Asia." Her voice was solid with conviction. "It's a thread from back when these hills had all kinds of ancestral species, radiating all over the world. Unifying us all these millions of years later."

"You know I'm down: 'Power Couple' is worldwide! You've always been a true believer when it comes to that stuff. Anyway, carry on. What about all these little things, the sensors?"

"Ok, well, the sensors will be recording all day. Then the big unit will download the data in a short burst back to my local SD card, and simultaneously send it out to the cloud on the satellite link. And voila, no need for any bulky battery pack for constant power. And the signals will only be detectable for a few seconds per day. So, if the network gets in place now near the creek, we will have near-constant datasets for the forest's stream flow, turbidity, pH, dissolved oxygen, heavy metals, and," Grace was staring intently at the large steel and yellow device, suddenly self-conscious of her focus. "And, maybe it can be enough to document and save a very old forest—and get me the publication I need for grad school!"

"Alright, let's get back to it, then! Ready, break!" Jay stood up and helped Grace set up the large central unit on the ridgeline overlooking the holler below.

"Okay, that's the last one. Canopy, soil, streams. All sixty-four of 'em are in place, and Two-Fork Creek is officially under observation for my— Wait! Oh shit!" Grace hissed. "Get down!"

Jay stood still, looking up at her in the tree, refusing to be intimidated. He rarely saw her scared out in the woods, and decided he was going to lean into his big protector role. It was approaching dusk, and though the sun was beneath the ridge of hills surrounding the holler, the sky was not yet dark. But the lengthening shadows in the bottom of the hollers always got darker earlier, and it was still hard to see. Grace and Jay had wound their way through the forest from the ridgeline, placing sensors as they went.

The creek had carved out the valley to give its name, having two branches, each of which forked off in their own directions. Neither had any trails over the ridge. The valley's ridgeline was obvious, a self-contained watershed. Hiking across forests and hills was the only way they could access the valley without going through the main road on the other side—the side where the landowner would likely be observing. It had been more than a six-mile trek to avoid detection.

"Jay! Seriously! Get down!" Her voice suddenly registered to him for what it was. Not just fear; urgent need and desperation.

His gaze followed hers towards the downstream end of the large rushing creek. Coming up the overgrown trail was a pair of headlights.

"But what about you?" Jay could see her in the branches of the sycamore, more than twelve feet up, having just zip-tied the last of her sensor boxes on a tree limb.

"I'll stay up here out of sight. I don't have time to get down. You hide! Go!" Grace was right, and he nodded in agreement. High up in the branches was not the first place people looked usually for trespassers, and Jay was not exactly hard to miss at his size. Grace winced as she watched Jay move as quiet as he could back through the underbrush wearing one of his WVU shirts that still had a patch of bright yellow on it. She, on the other hand, was petite and dressed in all earth-tones. Jay hunkered down just at the edge of her line of sight behind a fallen tree covered with a rhododendron.

The pair of headlights came closer. The vehicle's lights jumbled sporadically as it went over the uneven ground. Grace saw it emerge from the trees; it was a side-by-side ATV. Straight on, the lights were too bright to see through, but as it passed, her eyes adjusted enough to make out the passengers. Two men sat in the front seats, and a third rode standing on the back cargo bed. To her horror, the vehicle stopped only ten yards in front of the sycamore she clung to. Even directly below would have been better, as their range of vision would be looking away and outwards. At this distance, the passengers in the side-by-side would not even need to look up forty-five degrees and make eye contact with her.

The vehicle turned slightly to face the creek in the center of the valley, so Grace was not directly in the light cast by the bright LEDs. The creek was over fifty feet across, but not more than three feet in depth with a few deeper pools here and there. The valley was flat enough on the bottom, but overgrown with ferns and bushes, covered by a thick canopy above of sycamore, tulip poplar, and a few oaks. It was there in the overgrowth that the passengers got down from the muddied vehicle.

That's him! Martin Whaley! Grace recognized as she saw the landowner himself strut out, now visible in front of the headlights. She shuddered, thinking of her unpleasant interactions with him over the past few weeks trying to get her study approved. Rather than stay on the far side of the tree, Grace sensed that any conversation he might be having out here would be critical intelligence—whether for her research in the long term, or just for trying to make it out of Twin-Fork undetected. She inched around the sycamore trunk, balancing with her hand on a higher branch to get a better acoustic angle for eavesdropping.

"...and that's when I saw it on my trail cam. It just sent me a notification when we were going over that paperwork back at the cabin. There are two people out here. Just a few minutes ago." Whaley spoke to the other two, still in the dark behind the headlights.

"Are you sure it was her? Could it just be some hikers or something?" The other voice was a man, seated in the passenger seat. There was an undercurrent of nerves in the urban timbre of the voice.

"Well, usually, I don't think I could be sure. They all look alike to me, ya know? Black hair, squinty eyes. But this one, Blankenship, if I remember the name. Well, she was the one who done called me out of the blue. Remember we did the video call at your office? She's the one who had the gall to ask me about supporting some environmental bullshit on my land. It was all the usual stuff: coal is bad, blah blah blah. I told her no, but she emailed me a half-dozen more times trying to get me to change my mind. About *my* own land! That's just the problem with these types. They think science means they can violate my constitutional rights to make money on my property. They're afraid of coal jobs coming back to our state!"

"Oh, I can assure you, Mister Whaley, our company is very interested in your land and we know how to deal with *this type* of problem. My legal team specializes in protecting people like yourself from the meddling of interlopers who would try to stop you from profiting off an asset that you rightfully own." The man got out of the side-by-side passenger seat, joining Whaley in the harsh light. His accent was clearly from out of state. He had apparently not planned to be outside, as his white dress shirt had the sleeves hastily rolled up, and he stepped gingerly in his derby shoes through the brush.

"Yeah, you say that, Phil, but you also promised you would handle things at the office for approvals. And guess where this little Asian girl got my number from? From the regulator's office! Your people aren't doing their job. I said I did not want to have to deal with any site visits!" Martin Whaley turned, a big man himself, and stared down the slender man in the fine suit.

"Mister Whaley, as the company's representative on legal matters, I can assure you: even if an official site visit happens, we will know in advance. That contingency is why my associate, Mr. Thorpe, is here. He is very thorough, and will make sure any evidence of 'obstacles' to our operations will be removed before oppositional documentation can be made." To Grace, Phil's euphemisms only made him seem that much more sinister.

And Grace knew exactly what he was talking about: if the presence of an endangered species was found on land slated for development, the unscrupulous kind of developer would go in, find the endangered species, kill it, and destroy any evidence of it being there—nest, carcasses, anything. That way there would be no legal obstacle to anyone's operations. Grace had read about plenty of cases where that had supposedly occurred, but the lack of evidence—meaning the non-presence of an endangered species—made proving it all very difficult in court. As such, the justice system was powerless, and corporations remained undefeated. *That's where my work comes in! The missing piece!*

On cue, another man whom Grace assumed to be this 'Mr. Thorpe' stepped out to join the other two in the visible cone of the headlights. He was as big as Whaley, but younger and in obviously better shape—*though no match for my Jay.* Grace smiled at the thought of anyone in a physical contest with her Division I boyfriend. But her heart sank into freezing water when she saw that the man had a pistol strapped to his hip and a rifle on his shoulder. She swallowed hard, thinking about how local police in an area like this might see the case: *a local landowner and friend stood their ground and shot a trespasser, who happened to be black and very 'intimidating'. And the other one on their side was a lawyer, too! Just great!*

This was not how she had planned it. Things were suddenly much more complicated. *Maybe we should just come out now, apologize and go home,* she gulped at the thought, *with a misdemeanor on my permanent record. Yeah, the research ethics panel is going to love that. But still, I don't want to risk anything worse!* Grace looked at weapons slung on the third man, and began to doubt that misdemeanor charges were ever on the table. Big money always had a way of raising the stakes for people.

Then the conversation caught her attention again:

"Your man, Thorpe, he better be careful, though. My grandpa always said there was a mud-cat devil of some kind out there." For the first time, Martin Whaley's voice had lost a portion of its arrogance. "It killed two of his dogs one night. And our horses always spook out on Two-Fork, even the best trained ones."

"Mr. Whaley, I can assure you, local legends don't scare away outsiders anymore. We are practical people. I'm sure your grandpa had his reasons for those stories, even if they are just superstition. I don't blame people for their lack of education, as long as they know when to cooperate." The lawyer spoke, as if it was the last word on the topic, and turned to climb back into the passenger seat. "Now, let's continue, and see if we can find your trespassers. Then we can go back and finalize the paperwork for the mineral rights transfer."

"Boss, you want me to turn on the new receiver?" Thorpe called out gruffly as he hopped back in the ATV bed. Grace could hear his rifle clatter on the plastic bed liner as he pulled up something that looked like a radio receiver.

"Yes. Do it. You know how these college kids are with their phones. It's the best way to track them." The lawyer turned to Whaley: "Having the right equipment makes it all so easy."

Grace could see the man with the guns in the back pull out a device with an antennae and connect it to his smartphone. *He's going to try and find us with our signals? Like a bluetooth or wifi ping?* Her mind raced. She could turn off her phone, but that would leave Jay readily detectable. Her sensor network would not have any connectivity detectable at this time, only needing a daily burst of data transmission. Her boyfriend's phone would be the only signal in the holler—and he was a very short distance away. That confrontation was the last thing she wanted to happen. *Think, Grace, think!*

That's it!

Grace had not yet uploaded the schedule code to her sensors for transmitting data bursts. That would have been their next step before the interruption. For now, the sensor network was still on standby. She pulled up her own phone, the app she used for data collection was still connected to her big central unit that she had left on the top of the ridge, the best place for signal. As quick as she could type one-handed without losing her balance, she tapped the command to initiate data uploads: *function, (data upload(LOOP)): random (100, 10000) milliseconds; parameter (signal frequency (loop)): random (500, 50000) Mhz.* And just like her test run, she saw the text appear: *COMMAND RECEIVED.*

The chaos of RF frequencies was enough to buy some time. She hoped.

"Uh… Boss, something's weird." Thorpe scratched his beard. "I had two signals here in our vicinity. They started that way. But then we got some big signal and lots of little static."

"I told you that you should have let that FBI guy calibrate it for you." The lawyer, Phil, sounded disappointed. "He was too nervous selling us his government-issued gear, I guess. Got too rushed."

"Phil Sterling, the man who can't keep a lid on things, eh?" Whaley spoke with contempt. "You promised me I'd get paid after next week. I expect that to happen, or I'm going back to LeeCo's offer."

Grace's thumbs worked furiously through the app, trying to make the most of her borrowed minutes before the sensor networks' limited batteries ran out. Typing code on her phone's screen was always a pain, but one-handed, while hanging on for dear life was definitively the worst. She finally hit send, and prayed for the syntax to not have any typos: *function (satellite upload(direct)); override (voltage safety); override (low battery warning); signal strength (999).*

COMMAND RECEIVED.

"No, wait!" Thorpe called out again. "I've got a signal. It's strong. Constant. A few other dots of static, but I think this big one is them."

"What does that mean?" Sterling's voice had much less of his lawyerly coolness now.

Grace had triggered one of her sensors further up the creek to the ridge, Sensor Forty-One. She told it to upload a constant data stream at full power to the central unit. A last ditch effort at misdirection away from Jay.

"Well, if I had enough *training time* on this device with that agent before he bugged out, I would know for sure. My best guess is maybe it means the device I'm picking up is making a phone call right now. The data stream is about the right size." Thorpe shrugged and shook his head.

"They could be telling someone outside about something they found here. Maybe uploading photos?"

"Shit!" Whaley and Sterling said in unison.

One rushed scramble of a side-by-side motor later, and after a few minutes to ensure they were really gone, Grace finally took a breath.

Grace was picking a path of branches down the tree when Jay rushed out of the brush to her.

"We gotta go! Now!" Jay wore an expression she had never seen before.

"Yeah, no kidding! But, I think I bought us enough time. I'll have to explain what I did, but, trust me, I'm pretty much a genius! Though we can't use the same trail to leave. They might-" Grace was confident it would be at least another twenty minutes before they even made it to Sensor Forty-One, and then figure out exactly what was going on after that. But Jay interrupted her triumph.

"Not them. Something. Something *else!*" Jay looked at the stream off to the side, his eyes scanning back and forth. Grace's adrenaline was already high, but that was terror she saw. There was a growing confusion: Grace could not imagine what would spook a man of Jay's size and strength.

"Are those guys back? Are there others?" Grace's voice was low. "Uh, a bear?"

He shook his head at each suggestion.

Unsure of what to say next, she decided on action: "Well, come on, let's head south to follow the stream, then we can double back east and make it to the campsite parking lot by sunrise." She made one check on her own backpack and took one last look at her phone compass.

Grace tried to take a step south towards the creek, but suddenly felt a huge quivering grip on her shoulder.

"No." Jay stood still, and slowly released his hand, eyes still on the creek water as it swirled in the settling dark. "Go. Just *go.*"

Both of them snapped around in an instant as they heard a sound. Gunshots rang out further up the valley. Jay grabbed Grace's wrist and they ran through the dark.

"You sure you can't tell me whatever it was, Jay?" Grace stopped and looked down onto one of the forked branches in the valley below. Jay had led them to swing around north to make it back to their vehicles at the campsite parking lot rather than take the easier way south across the stream. The lights of Whaley's side-by-side were still visible far below. There had been a few smaller pops of pistol fire followed by two larger sounds of a rifle. Grace was not sure if she had heard screams or not. Jay was certain he had. But that had been more than an hour ago, and they agreed it was wiser to get away from the scene.

Jay was silent, his eyes saucer-wide in the moonlight, as he stared at the unmoving headlights in the forest below and shook his head.

"Do you want to talk about it? I know it was intense. I'm sorry. Really. I should not have come here at all, and I shouldn't have asked you to do something here that could get us in trouble with the cops or get shot at." Grace placed her hand on his arm.

"It's ok. It's not your fault." Jay finally smiled at her.

"Well, yeah, it kinda is my fault. I'm the one who asked you for help." Grace grimaced.

"Yeah, you right. You right," Jay laughed quietly.

"I can't help but feel a little sad that I got all the sensors in place but won't get a full data set. I think I burned out one of them when I sent those guys on that wild goose chase. The first bit of water quality data from Sensor Forty-One was, honestly, absolutely pristine. It's so sad that this whole water catchment area will be ruined when they strip these hills. I even overheard the landowner, Whaley, talk about hellbenders in the stream."

"Hellbenders?" Jay's eyes widened again.

"It's an endangered salamander. The biggest around here, actually. And they really depend on good water quality. One colloquial name for it is 'mud-devil', because it's so ugly." Grace referenced the term she had overheard, though she hardly believed that one could kill a dog.

"That's what I saw!" Jay nodded intently, suddenly opening up. "A big salamander."

"Really? In the dark? Is that why you were so shook up?" It was Grace's turn to be confused.

"You said it's big and ugly. It was very big. And very ugly!" Jay held out his massive arms in a large circle. "*This* big around."

Grace's confusion was increasing: "No, Jay. Hellbenders aren't more than three feet long, definitely not *that* big around." Her firm scientific foundation had to correct these irrational fears, she knew.

"Grace, I swear. The thing was just across the stream from me when I hopped behind the log to hide. I saw it. Its eyes were reflecting dull blue from the headlights, like a dead fish looking at me, and I could see all the slime along its back. And, the teeth! If you hadn't tricked those guys into leaving, I think it was coming for me. I ain't about to get eaten by that thing. I'd sooner run out and get shot! But when I got out of the bank, I guess it realized I was out of reach and just slid back into the water, like a gator or something."

Grace looked him full in the face, examining. She did not think he would pull a joke at a time like this, but wanted to be sure. Pulling out her phone, she sighed in relief when she saw there were two bars of signal still available. A few seconds of googling later, she turned her phone around to Jay and pointed: "Just to be clear: you're telling me it was like this?" Grace held the phone with one hand.

"Grace! See? I told you it was a hellbender! That one definitely ain't no three feet!" Jay was peering closely at the image on the screen.

"Jay," Her voice was slow and clear, "This picture is not a hellbender. This is an extinct species of giant salamander. Literally older than dinosaurs. That type would have been the largest predator in the world at its time. Its ecological niche was eventually filled by crocodilians, though it was much later when reptiles evolved."

"Grace, I know what I saw. And it was not a gator or a crocodile. I've been on the line of scrimmage enough to know when somebody is about to come at me, trying to break me. And that *thing* was!" Jay's voice was now more than a little defensive. "I know what I saw."

"Alright, alright. Sorry. It's just that, if you're right, you're saying that a living fossil has been in these hills for almost two-hundred million years." Grace let her words sink in.

"You said yourself, the mountains and old hollers were like a refuge for species from times past, right?" Jay held up a contradictory finger.

"Yes, but, we would have seen something of that size by now!" Grace protested.

"And you said most of Appalachia's environment has been disturbed, especially the water quality that affects salamanders? So the bad environment may have killed off most of them? Except for a place with 'pristine' water?" Jay pointed back down to the valley.

"Yeah, though—"

"And, since it's too cold up here for alligators, those salamanders could hibernate in the winter and still keep their niche." Jay smiled, as he saw Grace's eyes light up. She suddenly caught on to the thrill of possibility, a brush with death and the law be damned.

"Yes! And that same period of settling killed off the wolves and such, so there would be plenty of deer for a large carnivore, especially a cold-blooded one, to go unnoticed with minimal impact on their prey populations. Jay! This actually makes sense. If this is real, it would be more than just grad school. We could even get to name a species! Like the hellbender, *cryptobranchus alleganiensis*, but," She paused in thought, "Maybe: *cryptobranchus infernifractor?*"

"Uh, the what now?" Jay's smile paused midway.

"It's a play on words. Bend and—you know, never mind. Later. But, first, we would have to get documentation. And my sensors don't have cameras." Grace suddenly got a chill down her spine again as she looked back down the valley, thinking of any more possible confrontations with greedy landowners, corporate lawyers, or private security.

"Didn't you say that Whaley mentioned trail cams, like for tracking deer?" Jay suggested.

"Jay! You're a genius again!" Grace kissed his cheek. "We could copy his cam's SD cards maybe? But I'm not in a rush to go back down there yet. Not when Whaley and company are so close here. See? The lights are still on from their side-by-side. Hmm, maybe I need to get a drone?"

"Grace, I thought you just apologized for even doing this. But now you wanna go back? Why not just check your sensor network? There could still be something. Maybe they didn't even find Sensor Forty-One. Wasn't that one near the creek bank also?" Jay always knew this was his real role: not 'big protector,' but 'voice of reason.'

"Yeah, I guess. But I'll think of something, a better way next time. But you were pretty convinced you saw something—something huge! A possible living fossil! It could be a ground-breaking discovery!" As she spoke, she closed the images on her phone: eryops, prionosuchus, gaiasia. Her thumbs then moved in a flurry across the screen, typing in more commands on her sensor control app: *DISPLAY (Data, 41)*.

Then she froze.

This time, it was Grace's eyes that widened. "Sensor Forty-One sent one last data burst. It was just after we heard those gunshots, if the timestamps are accurate." Her eyes squinted, looking closer: "But, this reading is weird. Very weird. Some are still normal, still pristine. All except this one."

"Isn't it just environmental information?" Jay looked down again at the headlights on the side-by-side deep in the valley. He could have sworn it flickered, as if something moved in front of it.

"It was the chemical sensor reading. For the water quality, normally used for picking up heavy metals from mining waste." Grace's brow knotted in concern.

"Huh? I thought you said this place was, you know, *pristine*?" Jay now also scrunching his brow in thought.

"It is. All except the iron content. There is no machinery or mining discharge, obviously. It's such a weirdly high concentration of dissolved iron in the water. But what in the world would give a reading like this? It's not like it's…" Her expression paled with the realization, and her eyes reflexively looked back down to the faint lights on the ATV below, "Like *blood.*"

Grace and Jay stared down at the silent valley from on top of the ridge. Far below them, the electric headlights of the vehicle below flickered once, twice, and faded into black, leaving Two-Fork in darkness.

IN THE MINE

By B. B. Nott

THERE WAS SOMETHING in the mine. Elias Garrison knew it. Everyone in Mineral Creek knew it. Shit, anyone who had ever had the misfortune of even hearing about Mineral Creek knew it.

None of this concerned Elias much, even though he was a miner. *Everyone* in the small town of Mineral Creek was a miner, except for the women, who were all miners' wives, and the children, who were all miners' sons and daughters. Elias had been a miner's son once upon a time, and he'd grown up to be a miner, as was the way of things in Mineral Creek.

Elias was perfectly content with his life. He woke up every morning and ate breakfast, kissed Diana, kissed J.J. on the head, before leaving for his shift at the mine with a lunch that had been packed lovingly by Diana. He worked until his shift ended, at which point he always felt so tired that he felt if he took a wrong step his legs might collapse underneath him. Then he came home to a bath and a hot meal, both of which he savored, before he sat down on the couch to watch whichever late night show Diana turned on while he rested his eyes before going to bed at a respectable hour.

Or, at least, Elias *had* been perfectly content with his life, until J.J. had failed to have the good sense to keep himself alive.

He wasn't *dead*, at least not officially.

Diana had called Elias in a panic when J.J. hadn't come home. He'd told her he was probably just taking the long way home through the woods.

He hadn't been home when Elias had gotten home, either, and that's when they'd called the school. It had taken a while, but Principal Elkins knew the school bus driver's husband, and he'd called her, and they'd learned that J.J. had never gotten on the bus that day. He'd said instead he wanted to walk home.

Diana had said that they'd better call the police, in that tone of voice she always used when she was trying not to cry.

Elias had agreed.

When they'd called the police, the chief of police and an officer had come down to the house. Mineral Creek was a small town, and the police force was only a few men.

The chief of police seemed unconcerned. "Boys that age, they like to wander," he'd said, clapping Elias on the back as though they were friends. They'd sent out a search party to search for the 11-year-old, if only to placate Diana, who, by that point, was hysterical about the whole thing.

Elias knew better. J.J. wasn't the wandering type. He was a quiet, curious child, the kind of child who came home with a book thicker than the phone book every week checked out from the school library. A few years back, when he'd been in third grade, his teacher had called him and Diana in for a meeting, and said it might be better if they advanced him a grade. He already knew all the material she was teaching them.

Diana had thought it was a good idea, but Elias thought he ought to be with kids his own age. He had a better chance of fitting in that way.

Not that it mattered. He hadn't fit in either way. He was always the kid no one invited to birthday parties. Not bullied, not as far as Elias knew, but not included, either. He was the kid on the sidelines reading a book at recess.

Elias knew where J.J. was, though he hadn't told anyone. After all, who would he tell?

J.J. had gone after whatever was in the mine.

He'd been reading a book about aliens, and he'd been asking Elias about what was in the mine. Said he'd heard stories from kids at school, who'd heard stories from their daddies and granddaddies. Elias had heard the stories, too. He'd never told J.J. the stories because Diana was afraid they'd give him nightmares.

Instead, Elias had told him there wasn't anything in the mine that wasn't supposed to be there. Which, in a way, was true—whatever happened to be down there had probably been there since before Elias's granddaddy held a pick for the first time.

He'd told him not to worry his little head about it, and tussled his hair, and J.J. had laughed. Elias had made the mistake of assuming J.J. had forgotten the idea after that.

He'd gone missing two days later, and the only things missing from his room were a backpack, a flashlight, his library book about aliens, a map of the Mineral Creek mine system that he'd made at the library with his own pocket change and, most importantly, himself.

Elias knew the odds. He'd heard them on a news story a while back. Kids that went missing didn't come back on their own, not usually, and the longer it was, the less likely it was that they were alive. And there was plenty of dangerous shit down in the mine.

After the police had called off the search party for the night, Elias went down into the mine. At the kitchen table, he'd filled a backpack with things he thought he might need—rope, extra batteries for his flashlight, a pocketknife, and a dark chocolate bar, one of the nice ones Diana had given him for Christmas. Chocolate was J.J.'s favorite candy, and Elias's grandmother had always said there wasn't any problem that chocolate couldn't fix. He wasn't so sure she was right anymore, but he'd brought it along anyway, just in case.

As he stood up from the table, Diana stopped him, handed him two jelly sandwiches wrapped in foil.

"He's probably hungry," she said. There was a desperation in her tone that was so thick Elias could have wrung it out of her tone like a rag.

He'd taken the sandwiches.

The last thing he'd grabbed before he left was his grandfather's antique pistol from the gun safe. He'd waited until Diana had gone back upstairs to get it. She'd never liked that he had it; she always pursed her lips unhappily whenever she looked at the gun safe. He didn't want to have to use it. He didn't want to have to use the pistol. But there were some things he didn't know how he'd go on living after seeing. And it was better to be prepared for anything. He'd learned that long ago, when he'd been in the Scouts. He'd wanted J.J. to join the Scouts too, but his son had cried the whole night during his first camping trip, and Diana had insisted that he couldn't go back. She coddled him too much.

There was only one mine that J.J. could have gotten to without anyone seeing. One of the old mines had been closed off years ago, back when Elias was still in school. It was the kind of abandoned place that teenagers viewed with fascination and horror. Elias remembered being dared to step inside back when he was young and foolhardy. They'd boarded the entrance up, but that hadn't stopped anyone before. It certainly hadn't stopped him.

There was a sign that read 'Do Not Enter' on the front of the mine. The boards had fallen—or been pulled down—and there was a space just big enough for Elias to squeeze into.

He entered the mine, ignoring the sign. It looked like the same mine he worked in, raw stone walls with wooden beams crossing the ceiling and floor. It smelled different, almost stale somehow. The shadows his flashlight cast on the walls were long and eerie.

"J.J.?" he called. The only reply was the echo of his own voice.

The ladder down into the main depths was metal. The metal was cool on his fingers as he descended into the deeper and darker part of the mine.

The darkness was a presence all its own. The flashlight tucked under his arm did little to stave it off. The only sounds he heard was the sound of his own breathing.

He missed the safety of the mine he worked in, the lights always lit and the familiar background noise of the mine train that took him and the rest of the workers down into the depths. It was rattling and old but *safe*. This mine, with the silence and the darkness and the ladder that was probably older than Elias himself, felt almost hostile.

He'd never been down in a mine by himself before, and something about it felt strange and haunting. He'd watched a special a while back, about something called sensory deprivation tanks, where someone floated in a dark, quiet tank. The idea had given him the willies.

The mine felt kind of like that now.

"J.J.?" he called again. There was no reply.

Elias saw something skittering out of the corner of his eye, further down the tunnel, just out of sight of his flashlight's beam. *Probably a mine rat*, he thought.

He stood stock still; waited a long beat to see if it would run by again.

Whatever it was ran by again.

Elias pulled the sandwich out of his bag, tearing off a piece of bread. He threw it vaguely in the direction of the rat. There was a thought in the back of his mind that he couldn't stop tugging at, like a loose thread on a sweater, that urged him to lure it into the light, to make sure that it was only a rat and nothing more.

He watched as a strangely human hand crept out of the shadows, grabbing the bread. Rats didn't have hands like that, he was pretty sure.

Then again, he'd never seen a rat's paw up close. Maybe they did look like strange little human hands.

There was a strange feeling in his gut. He ignored it. He hadn't had dinner; they'd been too caught up in looking for J.J. to eat anything. He was probably just hungry.

He threw another bit of bread in the direction of the rat, this time a bit bigger.

This time, when the rat grabbed it, it came fully into the light.

The hairs on the back of Elias's neck stood up.

Whatever it was, it sure as shit wasn't a rat.

The thing—whatever it was—resembled E.T., except it had all of E.T.'s terrible qualities and none of its charm. E.T. had been J.J.'s favorite movie ever since it had come out last year. He'd made them take him at least three times to see it in theaters and had nearly cried when he got the VHS for his birthday.

It had big black wet eyes, the kind of eyes that shimmered in the dim light almost menacingly. Its skin was gray and mottled, and if Elias hadn't just seen it dart forward to grab the bread, he'd've thought it was a trick of the light, some kind of oversized rock some kind of oversized rock that just happened to look unsettlingly like a creature. It had large ears that made the creature appear top-heavy, as though it was going to topple over at any moment. It wore a pair of oversized, crudely constructed overalls that puddled on the mine floor underneath it.

Its fingers were long and unsettling, a joint too many on each finger. He watched as it tore the bread in half and then shoved it into its mouth.

It looked up at him. There was an expression painted across its face that looked almost like fear for a brief moment.

"Thank you," it said. Its voice was deep and gravelly, thick with an accent just like Elias's own.

Elias blinked.

He hadn't expected it to *talk*. He resisted the urge to pinch himself. He didn't need to. He must've been hallucinating, or dreaming, or something. Maybe there was some kind of gas leak, and that was the real reason the mine had been abandoned. Maybe he was experiencing some kind of hallucination due to the heartbreak. He'd heard of that happening before—a widower who kept seeing his wife around every corner, a mother who saw her dead daughter tucked neatly into bed every night. He supposed it didn't really matter, in the end.

"You're welcome," he said, his mouth forming the words before he could process that he was having a conversation with whatever this was.

It stared at him for a long moment, as though it was expecting something. The feeling of its eyes on him made Elias's heart race.

"Do you want some more?" he asked, mostly because he had no idea what else he was meant to say. He swallowed hard.

It nodded. "Yeah," it drawled.

Elias tore off a piece of the sandwich and tossed it toward the... whatever it was.

"Thank you," it said again, before devouring the bread at an almost concerning speed. If J.J. had been eating that fast, Diana would have made her trademark squawk of concern and told him to stop eating so quickly before he choked.

"What are you?" Elias asked, the words falling out of his mouth before he could stop them. The voice of his grandmother rang in his head: *curiosity killed the cat.*

"What are you?" it echoed back at him, still with a thick-accented masculine voice.

Its ears twitched, as though it heard something that Elias couldn't.

Something about the way its ears moved made Elias remember the stories his grandfather had told him.

Elias tore off a piece of the sandwich and tossed it toward the... whatever it was.

Elias had always looked forward to going over to his grandparents', because there was always a chance that Grandpa would tell him a story. He'd tucked Elias in at night and he'd told him stories of the fair folk, the elves who lived under the hills and came out at night and danced, lithe and graceful, and the shapeshifting ones like the pookah, and the household ones like the brownie that had to be fed and appreciated for the work they did.

He'd told Elias that once upon a time, when he was a young man working in the mine, he'd seen a tommyknocker. Tommyknockers, he'd said, were little, gnome-like creatures that lived in the mine. They knocked on the wall when the mine was about to collapse. That was why if you were ever down in the mine, and heard knocking, you'd better run, his grandfather had said, and Elias had promised he would.

He stared at the creature. It wasn't quite how he'd pictured tommyknockers—he'd pictured something a bit more human than the thing in front of him, wearing crude overalls and devouring bread as though it had never eaten before.

"You're a tommyknocker, aren't you?" Elias asked.

The thing—the tommyknocker—looked up at him and blinked its wet eyes. "Sure as," it said.

"You know everything that goes on in the mine, don't you?"

The tommyknocker nodded. "I'm the one in charge down here," it said, and it was as it spoke that Elias realized exactly why its voice sounded strange. It was the voice of the foreman, Luke. Shit, Elias was pretty sure that he'd heard Luke say that exact thing before.

Was it just echoing things it heard? Elias wondered.

He shook his head. He didn't have time to worry about that, not right now.

"Do you know what happened to J.J.?" he asked. There was something in his chest, tight and taut as though something had gotten stuck there. Maybe he was dying, and this was all some kind of hallucination as his brain struggled to make sense of what was happening. He almost hoped so. It would be easier that way.

There was a long beat before the tommyknocker spoke. "You ought to be careful," it said, which, Elias noted with frustration, was decidedly not an answer.

"He looks like me, but smaller," Elias said, which was only partially true. J.J. had gotten his mother's eyes, and his mother's tendency to go pale as a ghost when startled.

The tommyknocker said nothing.

"He was wearing jeans, and a white tee shirt, and sneakers. And a red coat." Those were the clothes that his wife had said were missing from J.J.'s closet, the clothes that were listed on the missing posters that were plastered around town. Elias couldn't remember if he'd seen him in that outfit or not. He couldn't even remember if he'd said goodbye to his son that morning, if he'd kissed him on the head as he ate his cereal or if he'd just waved as he'd gone out the door.

A better father would know. A better father would have found him by now. A better father wouldn't be hallucinating a child from a fucking fairy tale.

The tommyknocker looked at him. It said nothing still, only blinked at him.

"Look," Elias said. Frustration was boiling in his gut, overflowing and turning into red-hot anger. "Can you just tell me if you've seen him?"

The tommyknocker looked at him, its ears twitching. He couldn't read the expression painted across its face, though it was clearly making one.

"Could we make a bargain?" The words came out of his mouth so quickly that they nearly tumbled over each other. They were out of his mouth by the time he could consider if this was a good idea or not.

The men in the fairy stories his grandfather had told him were always making bargains.

They were always getting turned into animals or made to dance until they died of exhaustion or staying in the fairy realm too long and wandering out after a hundred years thinking only a few hours had passed for not wording things carefully enough, too, but Elias was trying very hard not to think about that.

"A trade?" it asked, and there was something almost hungry about its tone then, as though it wanted to make a trade more than anything.

Elias nodded. "A trade."

"What've you got?" it asked. If Elias closed his eyes, he could almost imagine that he was at work, one of his coworkers standing in front of him. They all had that same thick accent, that same gruff voice. Shit, he had that same voice. It could have been his own voice the tommyknocker was mimicking, and he wasn't sure he'd know.

Elias propped up his flashlight on a rock and opened his bag. He hadn't come prepared to make bargains with fairy tale creatures. He'd come here to find J.J., whatever that happened to mean.

He rooted around through his bag. A pocketknife, some loose extra batteries for the flashlight, a rope, a screwdriver, a broken pencil, his grandfather's antique pistol, and the dark chocolate bar.

None of it was really ideal, but it would have to do.

He pulled the chocolate bar out of her bag. "Do you like chocolate?" he asked.

The tommyknocker sniffed, loudly—it sounded like a dog intent on getting the scent of something the dog thought was particularly appealing, like deer shit.

"You can have the chocolate if you tell me if you've seen him," Elias said.

"Deal," it said. Elias unwrapped the chocolate bar, slowly. The faint, bitter scent of the chocolate made his mouth water. It smelled like the kind of Christmas that Elias would never have again—with Diana laughing behind the camcorder, and J.J. eagerly tearing into his presents.

When the tommyknocker took the chocolate bar from him, their fingers touched. It felt remarkably like touching a frog, its skin not quite the right texture or temperature to be human.

He watched as it sniffed the chocolate bar again, long, desperate inhales, before taking a slow, tentative bite. It chewed purposefully, as though it was savoring it.

Elias wondered, vaguely, if the chocolate was going to kill it. What kinds of things could tommyknockers eat, anyway?

He very quickly decided that he didn't care. It was clearly intelligent; if it wanted to poison itself, that wasn't any of his business.

There was a long moment where the only sounds were of the tommyknocker eating. It was unpleasant to listen to, somewhere between a toddler too young to be aware of the noise it made as it ate and an eager dog.

Elias waited until it swallowed to ask. "Have you seen J.J.?" he asked.

"Yes," it said. It took another big bite of the chocolate bar. There was chocolate smeared all over its face, and Elias felt a sharp twist of pain in his gut at the memory of a younger J.J. As a toddler, he'd gotten into the chocolate chips when Diana was baking, and she'd found him with chocolate smeared all over his face, grinning proudly like he'd just accomplished the greatest thing in the world.

"Where?"

It shrugged. "That wasn't the deal," it said. It looked at him for a long time.

Still making eye contact, it rapped lightly on the floor of the mine. There was a light tapping sound, as though someone was knocking on a door with one knuckle.

Elias's veins ran cold. "Is there something wrong with the mine?" he asked.

The stories his grandfather had told him had also said that like their taller fair folk relatives, they were often tricksters. Miners whose lights went out before they should have, or who lost their tools even though they remembered exactly where they'd put them, well, that was the fault of the tommyknockers.

Elias swallowed hard, staring at the tommyknocker. *Surely it had to be joking, right?* He thought to himself. There was an unsettling feeling that had wormed its way into his gut and wouldn't leave.

"Is there something wrong with the mine?" he asked again, trying to sound as though he wasn't moments away from shitting his pants in fear.

The tommyknocker shrugged. "What do you think?" it asked.

"I think I should run," Elias said, which wasn't exactly true: in the moment, the only thing his brain could think was that he was afraid. He was suddenly, deeply aware that he was deep underground, with tons and tons of rock above him.

Elias very quickly realized that the tommyknocker sitting in front of him was not the only tommyknocker in the Mineral Creek mine.

There were a million wet beady eyes, all watching him. There was the sharp feeling of terror in his gut as he realized that he was outnumbered. The flashlight's beam wavered on the wall.

The tommyknocker grinned a strange smile. It was too wide, the gums of its teeth all visible. This, of course, meant that its teeth were visible as well. It had strange, sharp teeth that were crowded into its mouth.

If Elias didn't know better, he'd think that it was grinning. The tommyknocker opened its mouth. "Run!" it said, in a voice that wasn't the same as any of the voices it had used before.

No, the voice that came out of the tommyknocker's mouth was J.J.'s.

WOOL EWE SURVIVE?

By Beau Lake

Part I—April 1997

SARAH HAFFERTY STOOD over the kitchen sink, smoking a Marlboro cigarette. She tried to smoke outside—the dangers of secondhand smoke, you know—but she feared if she stepped out onto the back porch, the kids would destroy the house.

They were wild things, with perpetually windswept hair and a taste for destruction. Sometimes, she wished she could foist them off on a mother wolf, yearning for a litter of cubs to suckle. The thought made her chuckle, a puff of grayish smoke tumbling from her flared nostrils.

A chilly breeze trickled through the cracked window, ruffling the bangs she'd carefully sprayed into place. With a shiver, Sarah pulled the neck of her bathrobe closed. It was an ugly, quilted thing; a gift from her ex before...well, before he was her ex. Before he complained that she never tried anymore, that her stomach flab sagged over the waistband of her underwear. Never mind that it was his kids that stretched her out like an old crewneck.

A cold snap had fallen upon Sevierville, the grass covered in a thin patina of ice; the low-hanging clouds threatened another round of snowfall. An inch of accumulation over the weekend, if the weatherman was right.

The cigarette poised between her lips, Sarah turned on the faucet and began to wash up from breakfast. In the hour since the Haffertys had eaten, the Frosted Flakes seemed to have been cemented to the bowls. She had to use her fingernails to scrape it off. Sarah found herself wondering whether she had cornflakes barnacled to her stomach lining, impervious to the sloshing tide of milk and coffee therein.

"Let go!" Dennis shrieked from the living room, his toddler screech not unlike an ice pick driven between one's eyes. He was always yelling, his tinny voice shaking the eaves.

"You let go!" Holden countered. The second grader often insisted he was "grown" but he was easily riled up by his younger brother.

There was a crash and then an uneasy silence. Sarah turned off the tap to listen, plucking the cigarette from between her lips with damp fingers.

It was better to wait, to let them settle it, if they were able. One day, they wouldn't have her to act as their referee and—

Oh, Sarah, she admonished herself, *don't think like that. That's not a glass-half-full kind of thought.*

And, to tell the truth (and nothin' but the truth, so help her God), Sarah was dog-tired. There was a mountain of laundry on the dining room table to be folded, a carpet that desperately needed vacuumed, flower beds choked with weeds—wherever she looked, there was something to add to the 'to do' list. What she wouldn't give for a day—hell, an hour—with no kids and no chores!

She was just about to turn the faucet back on when Holden wailed, "Mooooo-ooooom!"

"For God's sake," Sarah muttered, stubbing the cigarette out on one of the dishes still waiting to be washed, ash commingling with solidifying egg yolk.

She found the boys in the living room, both unscathed but red-faced, angry tears streaming down Dennis's cherubic face. A lamp that had once been on the end table was now on the carpet, the shade torn and the ceramic base cracked. The edge and inside of the taupe-colored base was a startling white, like a wound just before it filled with blood.

As soon as he caught sight of his mother, Dennis turned on the waterworks. Holden only scowled. "What happened?" Sarah asked, aware of the heat flooding into her cheeks. The lamp was neither an heirloom nor a prized possession, but that didn't mean she was happy about it. It was another item to add to the to-do list, another trip to the K-Mart, another expense she didn't have the funds to cover. Money had been tight since their dad dove headfirst into his secretary's lap.

"Dennis pushed me," Holden explained, "and I bumped into the table."

"Just ... go play outside," Sarah said, flapping her still damp hands at them. "And keep your hands to yourselves."

"It's cold out there," Dennis whined.

"Put on a jacket," she snapped. "Now."

Dennis's face screwed up, whether to scream or cry, Sarah wasn't sure. "There's a monster out there. That's what Sam said at school. It..." He paused, his teeth dimpling his lip, "ate one of their lambs."

"Sam tells stories," Sarah said, unable to hide the edge to her voice. Dennis couldn't handle a scary story, even one told in good fun. He'd been peeing the bed a lot recently, and she had a sneaking suspicion it was all Sam's fault. What had Dennis said when he crept into her room, his pajama pants damp and hanging off his hips? "I was scared of the white thing, mama, it sometimes gets confused and eats little boys, thinkin' they're lambs."

If only she could wring Sam's little neck.

Holden snatched his brother's hand, dragging him to the entryway. "C'mon, Den," he wheedled, "let's go find some bugs."

"There are no bugs out," Dennis blubbered, though he let his brother slide his arms into the sleeves of his woolen jacket. "It's too cold."

Sarah's chest squeezed at the sight of them, Holden acting well beyond his six years. He'd had to, hadn't he? He was the man of the house.

"It'll be colder in here if you argue with mama," Holden assured him, pulling on his own windbreaker. "Let's go."

Quiet settled on the Hafferty house as Sarah picked up the pieces of the lamp, carrying them into the kitchen. She caught glimpses of the boys in the fenced-in yard, the purple stripe on Holden's windbreaker catching her eye as they flitted back and forth, playing some form of tag.

She quickly found that the lamp was beyond repair and threw it into the trash. When she returned to the dishes, she glanced out the window at the boys, expecting to see them squatting beside the wilting rosebush, looking for caterpillars.

But the yard was empty, the gate swinging with every gust of cold wind, a swath of purple nylon snagged on the latch.

She ran out back, only somewhat aware of the cold on her bare feet. "Boys?"

No answer.

Sarah strained to hear any sign of them: a tinkling of laughter, the squeak of a shoe on sidewalk, even the rustling of tree branches. They weren't supposed to climb trees, but God, she'd be so relieved to find them up in the boughs of an oak now. She might not even scold them. "Holden? Dennis?"

The cold made her skin prickle, her breath catch in her chest. Sarah hugged herself, wishing she was hugging the boys she'd shooed out of the house, wishing she hadn't been so quick to admonish them. It was just a lamp. Just a stupid lamp.

In this moment, she wouldn't know it, but she'd condemned herself to a life of sitting in the dark. Alone. She would never buy another lamp, never change the bulbs in the ones she still had. What was the point?

And she would believe, with her whole heart, that monsters existed. Because something had taken her boys. If giving that something claws and ram-like horns gave her some peace, so be it.

A monster was far easier to stomach than the mugshot of the man with the baseball cap whom she'd once hired to mow her lawn.

Part II—April 1998

Eamon Miller had never been out-of-doors after nightfall. That was the rule at home: he was to come inside when the shadows lengthened, when the streetlights clicked on. But tonight, he was sitting on a log while his troop leader knelt beside a leaning teepee of logs.

"As our campfire smoke curls upward," Mr. Forrester recited, striking a match, "may all that is mean and unkind be carried away from our midst." Despite the burgeoning fire, peaked shadows loomed over the twelve boys in Troop Thirteen. They'd inadvertently erected the tents too close to the fire circle.

Eamon absently rubbed at the gooseflesh on his pale, knobby knees. He found himself unable to look at anything but the infant fire as it chewed up the kindling, growing larger with every subsequent gulp.

He had his fire safety badge and knew the danger, but it was less scary than the shadows. He didn't like these shadows—languid and inky, not pale and meek like the ones that fled when his Superman night light was switched on. These shadows leaned into the circle, their icy breath on his neck.

It's just a cold night, he assured himself, *and you are safe because you're at Camp Powhatan.* Still, it was so dark and he missed his mom. He wouldn't dare say so aloud. They were only kids, but just old enough to find missing their mommies—or having night lights—uncool.

"And in the friendly glow of our fire," Mr. Forrester continued as he stood back to admire his handiwork, "may peace and contentment wash over us all."

"Pfffft," James farted through wet, pursed lips, spraying saliva.

"Shhh," Eamon elbowed James in the ribs.

"Can we tell ghost stories?" James abruptly asked, undeterred by his friend's embarrassment. "I heard one about this girl who lives in your mirror."

"*Shhh,*" Eamon insisted, this time because he would like nothing less. He was already scared, even if he wouldn't admit it.

Just then, he became aware of an insistent twinge in his bladder. Eamon cast an apprehensive glance into the darkness, knowing the outhouses were out there. Somewhere. Could he hold it? Maybe if he stayed up all night, his knees pinched together, he could make it until sunrise.

Or he might wake up in a cold puddle, the laughingstock of Camp Powhatan. James, in particular, would never let him live it down, just like he never let James forget the time milk shot out of his nostrils. Such was friendship.

"Or—" James really was such a prick. "—how about the story of those two boys who disappeared last year? I heard a monster dragged them out here into the woods."

"You're stupid," Mickey shot out from the next log over. "They were murdered by some creep. That's why they made us watch that video about strangers in white vans at school."

Eamon's legs snapped shut, lest he dribble a bit of pee on his khaki shorts. James knew how badly that story scared him, how it kept him up at night even under the watchful eye of his Superman nightlight, his cat a warm, breathing lump against his hip. He'd seen the kids' faces in *The Mountain Press*, their features just indistinct enough to be anyone. He'd even read the article, haltingly sounding out the bigger words. The boys had disappeared from their own yard, hadn't they? If being surrounded by fences hadn't kept them safe, what hope did he have?

James had told him the kids had been eaten whole, their bones scattered across the Appalachian Mountains as the monster burped them up. "They found the littlest one's metacarpals—those are hand bones, Eamon—in a pile of old, molding hay in some holler up the ridge," he'd stage-whispered, cupping his hands around the clamshell of Eamon's ear.

"Settle down, James," Mr. Forrester said. He resembled a basset hound, his tired eyes half-hidden by drooping eyelids. It was as though he was surrounded by an unrelenting heaviness and, in fact, he was.

Namely, twelve eight-year-old boys, up well past bedtime.

"Is there really a monster?" The little voice came from across the fire and Eamon squinted to see who it was. Paulie. He was the smallest in their Cub Scout troop, shorter even than Eamon by a quarter-inch. Which they knew for a fact because they all had to measure one another for their personal fitness merit badges. Eamon still had the bruise on his wrist from where James had slapped him with an unguarded yardstick.

"Yeah," James answered, "and it loves eating the littlest boys. You and Eamon are toast."

Eamon could not push the image of the boys in the paper from his head. Despite the halftone dots, some smudged, he felt as though they looked just like him. Surely that meant the monster had a type: tow-headed boys with freckles and slightly upturned noses.

His anxiety, coupled with his need to pee, made him tremble. His teeth chattered.

James, apparently feeling the tremor of their log, gave him a sidelong look. "Are you alright?" he asked, serious now. His teasing was just in good fun, Eamon reminded himself, James loved him like a brother.

"I have to go," Eamon whispered.

"Go?" James's dark brow puckered in confusion. "Go where?"

"I have to pee," Eamon hissed.

"Oh!" At once, James' hand shot up. "Mr. Forrester! Eamon has to piss!" The fire circle erupted in giggles.

"Jay!" Eamon hugged his knees, his cheeks as hot as the fire.

"If you need to go to the restroom, go ahead," Mr. Forrester said kindly. "Take a flashlight."

"By myself?" Eamon squeaked. He cast a wary glance outside the fire circle, the shadows as impenetrable as a phalanx. They'd learned about the Spartans in World History, which was where he'd heard the word. It had stuck in his head like a catchy cereal jingle and he liked the feel of it in his mouth: the edge of his top teeth against his bottom lip (ph-), his tongue flicking against his hard palate (-la-), and finally, the push of air through the jail bars of his crooked teeth (-anx). Phalanx, phalanx, phalanx.

"James, go with him," Mr. Forrester instructed, "and no dilly-dallying. If you aren't back in five minutes, that'll be a demerit."

Eamon jumped to his feet, snatching the flashlight from his pack. He switched it on with his thumb as James rose more slowly, irritated that he'd been roped into this. "Fine," he grumbled, taking the flashlight from Eamon's hands. "But I'm holding the light."

Together, the two boys headed into the darkness, the flashlight's beam bobbing. The outhouses were a good hundred feet from the campsite proper and soon the campfire was a smudge of orange on the horizon. Dimly, Eamon could hear the chatter of his troop and the rumble of Mr. Forrester's laughter.

The flashlight's beam moved skyward, illuminating gnarled branches that resembled reaching hands, curved talons. At once, Eamon tripped over a root. "James, stop fooling around," he admonished his friend.

"Sorry." The beam returned to the uneven earth.

Soon, the row of outhouses appeared. "Go on," James said, gesturing with the flashlight. The beam briefly illuminated rough-hewn planks, a tin roof sagging under the weight of decaying leaf litter from the winter before.

"Give me the light."

"Fuck off!" James scoffed, free to curse now that they were out of earshot of Mr. Forrester. He loved to do whatever was considered adult or off-limits. He'd even tried to smoke one of his father's cigarettes, though he'd turned the color of pea soup and puked all over his New Balance sneakers.

"It's dark in there!"

"It's dark out here," James countered. "Go on."

Eamon considered fighting him for it, but James was not known to fight fair. He couldn't possibly win. "Fine," he grumbled, "but don't you dare leave me."

"I won't," James promised. Eamon hoped he was being sincere, didn't have his fingers crossed behind his back. He wanted to argue but now that he was near the outhouses, his desperation had increased tenfold. He needed to pee and he needed to do it *now*.

"Fine." There was no knob on the door, just a hole where one should be. Eamon opened it with a crooked finger.

Eamon found himself inside a stinking, black void, the light from James's flashlight barely trickling through the wooden slats. With his hands outstretched, Eamon felt for the roll of one-ply toilet paper, his knees bumping into the wooden bench with the hole in the center. He pulled down his pants and sat, not trusting himself to aim in the dark.

The flashlight strafed across the door and disappeared, plunging him into darkness. "James?" Eamon called nervously, keenly aware of the rough-hewn wood plank beneath his palms, the rattle of the tin roof as a crisp breeze slipped beneath the joists. "James!"

Something slammed against the wall to his left, making Eamon scream. He expected James to cackle in response to his reedy, girlish yell, but there was nothing. Just the wind. "Hello?" Eamon called.

Slowly, Eamon rose, pulling up his khakis. He was never good at putting on a belt, and it was harder with shaking fingers; he left it to dangle from the loops. "Jay?"

He pressed his face to the door, peering through the slats. His eyes had adjusted somewhat, and he could make out the dark shadow of trees. "James?"

No answer.

But he could hear someone—*something*—breathing. "James," he shouted, slamming his little fist against the door. "This isn't funny!"

From somewhere in the dark, came a wet gurgle. A moan. Eamon had never heard anything like it before. It didn't sound ... human.

And then: "Baaaa!"

The monster! The monster that James said ate those boys last year. "Don't be silly," he muttered under his breath, "monsters aren't real."

But between the darkness and that grotesque sound, Eamon found himself believing. He believed it with every fiber of his being.

"James?" He could only manage to whisper now, his voice stolen from him.

Surely Mr. Forrester would come find him. He and James had been gone too long.

Unless—

Unless the white thing had gulped down the members of his troop like he gobbled up the beads on a candy necklace.

A little whimper escaped Eamon as he retreated to the corner, curling up like a fawn left behind by its mother. He would wait, he decided. He would wait 'til morning or Mr. Forrester came for him, whichever came first.

Part III - August 2025

"What happened after?"

Eamon pulled his microphone closer, holding it with both hands as though it could serve as an anchor. Even now, 27 years later, he still felt a chill edge down the back of his neck when he told it.

The Supernormal Podcast recorded live in a small, rented office space, the walls plastered with B-movie posters. In the corner stood a life-sized Frankenstein's Monster animatronic, its arms outstretched and its eyes half-lidded. The hosts—Alice and Caleb—watched Eamon expectantly, their faces partially obscured by microphones and pop filters. They were both in their mid-twenties but, to him, they looked younger.

Like kids.

He was only thirty-five but felt ancient. His bones hurt and he walked with stooped shoulders. He kept his head on a swivel, always on guard. Even in the small room, he found himself eyeing the animatronic as if afraid it would come alive, despite its cord being unplugged.

"I fell asleep," he said, swallowing the lump of emotion in his throat. "When I woke up, the sun was up."

"Your critics find that far-fetched," Alice said with an apologetic look.

He'd expected this, but still his hackles rose. "Think of all the times kids think there's a monster in their closet. They hide under the blankets, resolving to stay awake, but they're just kids. Kids aren't built to stay awake all night, especially under duress."

"Yes, but this wasn't a monster in your closet," Caleb commented. "What did you see when you left the outhouse?"

"I..." Eamon's mouth felt as dry as the Sahara. He reached for the cup of coffee they'd given him, taking a measured sip. "I didn't see anything. James was gone."

"Gone?" Alice's brow furrowed.

"As soon as I came out, I was surrounded by people: Mr. Forrester, my troop leader, park rangers, police. They'd been looking for us, they said."

Eamon hesitated, balling his fists on his lap. His nails dug half-moons into his palms. "They searched for days—weeks—but never found him."

"And when you say 'him'?" Caleb prompted. Above his head, the LIVE sign glowed red. Red like the blood rushing through Eamon's ears, the bass drum of his heart keeping him on beat.

Eamon wanted to say, you know precisely who I mean. You just want me to say it. You just want to hear my voice crack, to get the sound bite. Instead, he played his part. "James."

They'd been best friends, James and him. They'd promised to be friends forever, even going so far as to shallowly cut their palms with a pocketknife and shake hands. That blood pact had held—Eamon kept people at arm's length now, hadn't had a friend since.

"You claim it's a monster that took him."

"I don't 'claim' anything. It was a monster—a white thing."

Caleb's eyes flicked to his notepad. "A so-called sheepsquatch. Surely you can see why people would doubt your story."

"You promised you would listen," Eamon shot out, spittle dappling the filter shrouding his microphone. "You said you believed me."

Alice shifted as if to reach across the table, as if to touch him. Eamon shrank away. "We just need to tell the whole story, Eamon," she murmured, so low that Eamon doubted the microphone could even pick her up. "Warts and all. You know about the allegations against James's stepfather, don't you?"

Eamon's tongue was 40-grit sandpaper. He gulped the remainder of his coffee even though it burnt all the way down. "It wasn't him. It was the white—"

It was Alice's turn to consult her notes, her auburn hair falling across her face like a curtain. "He's serving a sentence for child endangerment, sexual abuse."

"It wasn't him," Eamon insisted. He could tell that they were annoyed by him, by the story he wove. It meant the stitches of their own narrative were imperfect.

He was a loose end. A wiggling tooth in a child's mouth, worried by the tongue. Without him, it was a crime story and with him? Well, with him, it was a goddamn mess.

"I know what I saw."

"By your own admission, you didn't see anything," Caleb reminded him. "Just shadows."

Eamon winced. "Yes, but—"

"Some of the members of our Discord group," Caleb continued, "speculate that you had something to do with James's death."

"Me?" Eamon laughed. He couldn't help it. "If you really, truly believe an eight-year-old led his friend into the woods and killed him, we have nothing more to talk about."

Eamon rose, shoving the microphone away. It tipped, a high-pitched whine emanating through the headphones. He ripped the cans off his ears, letting them drop onto his empty chair. "Good luck with your show," he said curtly.

Outside, Eamon lit a cigarette and took a long, slow drag. His shirt stuck to the small of his back, the acrid smell of sweat commingling with nicotine and tar. The cicadas were out, their screams not unlike the screaming in his own head.

Going on the podcast was stupid. Of course they only pretended to believe him. Like everyone else, they thought he was a liar or, worse, a killer.

Slowly, he trudged to his pickup, dreading the drive home. The air conditioner didn't work and he would have to drive the whole way with the windows down. And what was there for him at home? An empty house, the television his only compatriot.

"Sir?" An older woman was waiting in the parking lot, leaning against a blue Acura. She had a pack of Marlboros and a Stanley cup on the hood, as if she'd resolved to wait there a long time. "Are you Eamon Miller?"

"Yeah?" Dimly, he could hear Caleb and Alice's voices over the Acura's radio, trying to right the ship he'd overturned when he left. Such was live radio.

The woman didn't look familiar, but he could swear he knew her. Or maybe it was the haunted look in her eyes—so much like his own.

"I'm Sarah Hafferty and I believe you. That ... thing ... took my boys."

THE LOST AND THE ROOTED

By Cecil Adkins

THE MOUNTAINS FELT smaller now. Smaller, but heavier. The road bent the same way it always had, sloping down toward Fairmont, the blacktop slick from a morning rain that hadn't quite burned off. The windshield wipers kept time with the curves, squeaking faintly at the end of each swipe. The smell of wet pavement drifted through the vents, sharp and mineral, like stone cracked open. The ridges seemed to press closer than he remembered, muffling sound, their trees dripping steadily in the silence between the engine's hum.

Nico kept one hand on the wheel and the other curled into a loose fist on his thigh. The hum of his engine wasn't the only hum in his head.

He had forgotten how West Virginia roads could twist so tight it felt like the mountains were folding themselves around you. Kudzu strangled fence posts even here in the northern part of the state, and coal trucks still barreled around blind curves like they owned the roads. As he neared his uncle's property, half the houses he passed sagged under tin roofs patched with tar, and the hollers—he shook his head at the common mispronunciation—still smelled faintly of woodsmoke even in summer.

Saul's house sat low in its *hollow*, the paint gone the color of old paper. Nico parked at the edge of the driveway where the gravel thinned into weeds. The screen door hung crooked, and if he didn't know better, he'd think the place was empty. As soon as he turned the knob and opened the door, though (Uncle Saul never locked his door during the daytime), Nico heard the hiss of the oxygen tank inside, loud enough to compete with the rain still ticking in the gutters.

It sounded like another hum, different from the one still in his head.

The air smelled like dust and burnt coffee. Saul sat in his recliner, the plastic tubing from his BiPAP machine looped over his ears, disappearing into the clear mask covering his nose and mouth. His eyes lit at the sight of Nico.

Saul pulled his mask below his mouth and rasped, "You made it."

Nico could almost feel the relief radiating from his uncle. Until a few days ago, Saul had been tended to night and day by a home health care nurse. When she'd broken her leg in a car accident, the agency said it might be a week or more before they could find a permanent replacement. Nico owed this man more than he could ever repay, so he took it upon himself to contact the agency and let them know he had it taken care of.

Now that he was here and could see Saul with his own two eyes, it was apparent that his uncle needed something other than simple health care.

Palliative care, thought Nico, *is what he needs now*.

He hoped he was up to the challenge.

"Yeah." Nico set his duffel by the wall next to the door and looked around the living room. Same wallpaper curling at the seams, same sagging couch with the cigarette burn in the armrest. He could almost see himself at ten years old, sitting cross-legged on the rug, waiting for Saul to come in from the garden. "Place looks the same."

Saul smiled faintly. "You don't."

Nico walked to the old desk in the corner, which was stacked with yellowed clippings, some curling at the edges. Police reports. Obituaries. Handwritten notes. A sketch in pencil and colored shading—a tall, thin figure with skin like wet leaves and bright yellow eyes. It was paper-clipped to a typed statement: *Vegetable Man sighting—June 1968.*

Nico remembered it. Remembered Saul showing it to him when he was a kid, telling him that not everything strange was dangerous. Back then, it had sounded like one of those things adults say to make you feel safe. The kind of thing his mother might have said, before she was gone. He had only fragments of her now: the lilt of her voice when she spoke Spanish on the phone to her sister in El Paso, the warmth of her hand against his hair as she tucked him into bed, the faint smell of cumin and lime that clung to her cooking. After she died, his father hadn't wanted the reminders. He hadn't wanted Nico, either. The memory of being dropped here—Saul's house, his bag shoved into his arms—was as sharp as the smell of rain still on his clothes.

By nightfall, the clouds had dropped lower, pressing down on the hollow. Nico lay in a newish bed in his old room, staring at the ceiling. Somewhere down the road, a dog barked, sharp and steady, angled toward the tree line. Then, silence.

He thought of his mother again in that silence, how she'd once told him that silence was never empty. It was always full of things people didn't want to say out loud. His father's silence had been full of shame. Saul's, full of tired love. This silence, here and now, pressed at him like a weight.

The hum in Nico's head was still there.

The next morning, the sky was the color of tin. Nico walked the trail behind Saul's property, his boots sinking into the damp mulch of last year's leaves. Mist still clung low to the hollows, silvering the briars, and every step sent up the smell of wet earth and leaf-rot. A woodpecker hammered somewhere far off, the sound echoing as sharp as nails into the stillness.

He told himself the walk was just to stretch his legs, to get air that didn't taste like dust and antiseptic. His knee ached from the injury he'd gotten during his very brief career as a college football player, but he left his walking stick behind. Sometimes the pain from his leg helped him focus less on things he didn't want to think about.

Like Uncle Saul's impending death.

The trail wound through second-growth woods, branches dripping from the night's rain. Moss clung to fallen logs, and the air smelled green and raw, like something that hadn't quite finished growing. A squirrel rattled down a trunk and scolded him before vanishing into underbrush. Somewhere farther off, water moved over rock, the creek swollen with runoff. This was the land his mother had tried to make her home in, even when neighbors looked at her like she was trespassing. She used to walk these ridges for hours with him when he was a boy, telling him that the woods didn't care where you came from, only how you treated them.

He'd come here to help the man who'd practically raised him through his final days, and he'd thought he'd be able to handle it just fine. He was still just a med student with another year or two of school to go, but he'd already seen a fair amount of death and suffering up close and personal. He usually had a pretty stoic view of the matter: all we have is today, and it's a gift, and what might (will) happen tomorrow doesn't change that.

Easy thoughts. Harder to put into practice.

The trail sloped down toward a narrow creek bed, swollen from the rain. The water moved fast, carrying bits of branch and leaf with it, and Nico found himself watching the current a little too long. It reminded him of childhood summers, floating sticks downstream and pretending they were ships going off to someplace better. Back then, Saul would tell him the mountains kept secrets, that not everything the creeks carried away was meant to be found again. Nico had always thought it was just a story, the way old men filled silences. But today, with the hum gnawing in his head, it felt more like a warning.

Half a mile in, something caught his eye: a smear of green on the edge of a broadleaf. Not moss. Too wet, too bright. He bent closer. The smell hit him before his fingers touched it: metallic, with a faint sweetness that stuck in the back of his throat. He wiped his hand on his jeans, ignored the sudden shock of tingling, almost pleasant pain that went from there to his bum knee, and kept walking.

The ache, which for years had been a steady throb in his leg, dulled almost instantly. He froze, hand still pressed against denim damp with green, and flexed his knee as if to test it. No pain. Just heat radiating upward, like standing too close to a fire.

The trail bent toward a line of maples where a storm, maybe yesterday's, had dropped a limb. It lay split down the middle, bark peeling back like curled paper. Something was caught in the shadows beneath it.

At first, he thought it was the remains of a deer, covered in foliage. But it was too long, and he could make out limbs that were jointed all wrong to be a deer. They bent sharp and thin, more like saplings than bone. The longer he looked, the less he could fit it into any shape he knew.

Then it shifted, slow, like it hurt to move. Nico could make out the hilt of a large knife sticking out from the creature's side.

It opened its eyes and looked at him.

Yellow eyes, like the ones in Saul's sketch. Skin the dull green of wet leaves, pulled tight over angles too sharp for bone. When it breathed, he heard it. It wasn't air, not quite, but a faint rasp like wind through stalks of corn. Its ribs rose and fell with shallow effort, and when it exhaled, the air smelled of copper and cut grass.

No mouth moved, but something hit the inside of his head. A single shape of thought, not quite words but close enough to understand.

Help me.

Nico stepped back. His pulse thudded in his ears. The smell of that green smear on his jeans was stronger now. It clung sweet and metallic to his tongue, impossible to swallow down. The hum in his skull quickened, matching the pace of his heartbeat.

He turned, started back toward the house. He made it ten paces before he noticed something and stopped. The hum, the one that had been in his head since he'd gotten within five miles of Fairmont, was louder here.

He turned around again.

The thing hadn't moved much. Its eyes stayed on him like it was waiting to see if he'd figured out who it was.

It was dark by the time he brought blankets to the root cellar. It was behind Saul's property and hadn't been used in years; the door had stuck halfway before it groaned open. Rust flaked off the hinges, and the smell inside was damp and mineral, like rainwater sitting too long in a metal pail. Cold air rolled up the stone steps, carrying a hint of mildew and old roots.

Nico had played here as a child, stacking Mason jars like blocks and daring himself not to flinch at the skitter of cave crickets in the corners. Now the place looked smaller, the stone walls weeping with condensation, roots pressing down through cracks overhead. It felt like the earth was trying to reclaim the room.

The thing was where he'd left it, wedged between the back wall and a broken shelf. Its eyes tracked him in silence. The shard of metal in its side caught in the lantern light, dull and slick with that green blood. The sight of it made his stomach tighten; the green wasn't just green. It shimmered faintly, the way gasoline slicks rainbow across a puddle.

Nico crouched. "This'll hurt," he said, unsure if it could hear words the way it sent thoughts.

He worked the knife loose, inch by inch. The blood clung to his gloves in threads, warm even in the cold air. The creature's body tensed but didn't pull away. When the shard came free, it gave a shudder that moved through its frame like wind through a sapling.

Images hit his mind in jagged pieces: trees burning, a sky the wrong color, the ground falling away. The sick lurch of impact. Then they were gone, leaving a faint static hum—that same damn hum—in their place.

It flinched when he shifted the lantern. Nico dimmed it, the shadows softening against the creature's face. The hum in his head eased with the light.

He tore strips from one of the blankets, pressing them against the wound. The fabric stained almost instantly, but the bleeding slowed in a way that felt almost intentional, as if the creature's body had decided it was willing to let him help. For a moment, Nico thought of one of his med school rotations when he met a few undocumented immigrants who had avoided hospitals until illness or injury forced them in. They'd been terrified someone would turn them in if they admitted where they came from. The look in their eyes wasn't so different from this one's.

Back at the house, Saul sat at the kitchen table, a coffee mug cooling in front of him. His gaze dropped to the green smear on Nico's pants. The creature's blood was still wet there, which should have been impossible. Surely there had been enough time for it to dry, but no. It was still wet and had seeped through his jeans. He could feel it on the skin of his thigh.

"You found it," Saul said. Not a question. "Just like I did."

Nico poured himself a glass of water, keeping his back to his uncle. "I found... something."

Saul gave a quiet laugh, then coughed until his shoulders shook. "Careful," he said when he caught his breath. "You start talking about it, they'll call you crazy, too. No matter how much truth you tell."

The rain came in thin sheets that night, needling the tin roof. Saul called Nico into his room after dinner.

The lamp by his bed threw more shadow than light. On the nightstand sat a folded newspaper clipping, edges soft with age. Saul tapped it.

"They said I made it up," he said. "Back in '68. Said I was drunk, or looking for attention. I knew what I saw."

Nico leaned against the wall.

"Vegetable Man. Or Veggie Man. That's what they called it in the stories that started spreading. But by that point, they'd said it was someone else who'd seen the thing and not me. Some fella named Frederick. Or maybe he *did* see it, and it was just his story that stuck. I never learned its real name, although I did ask it the second time. Tall as a basketball player, thin as a beanpole. Eyes like two coals, only yellow. Stood in the middle of the trail, just looking at me. I could only make out a few words that it... sent... into my mind, but even so. I knew it wasn't dangerous. Just lost. Looking for home. Or... a home." He paused, like the words cost him something. "The few that believed my story went out looking for it with pitchforks. Literally, in one or two cases."

The oxygen hissed. Rain hit the roof harder.

"They were good people, too," Saul went on, his voice rough. "At least, I'd always thought so. Neighbors, cousins. The kind that'd fix your roof if a storm tore it off, or bring food if you were laid up. But when something showed up they didn't understand? They turned mean fast. Fear'll do that."

Even if it's unjustified, Nico thought.

"It's probably an alien," Saul theorized. "It never told me as much, the two times I saw it. But it obviously wasn't from around here. Which is why the people with the pitchforks went after it."

Nico went back to the cellar. The creature was awake, eyes catching the lantern's glow. Moisture beaded on its skin like dew on leaves. Its chest rose and fell in slow, shallow pulls, and when it shifted, joints popped like green wood bending. Before he could speak, the visions hit, stronger this time. Shapes moving through a forest not like this one, shapes made of metal and light. Grabbing others like it, dragging them into the dark.

And then: a forest scene much more familiar to Nico. A very human-looking shape pointing a gun toward the creature. Another human, lunging toward it with a knife...

The panic in those images wasn't abstract. Nico felt the sharp stab of fear like it was his own, like he was the one being hunted. It reminded him of border-crossing stories he'd heard in free clinics—families who'd walked for days, who hid from men with guns and dogs. People who only wanted a safe place but were treated like invaders.

People like his own mother.

He pulled back, the smell of green blood sharp in his nose. "They're still looking for you," he said. "Here and... *there.*"

The creature's eyes didn't blink.

Nico thought of Saul's words. Not dangerous. Just lost. Scared. He set his lantern down, lower than before, and for the first time since he'd found it, the thing didn't look afraid of him.

The silence in the cellar grew thick. Water dripped rhythmically somewhere, every drop sounding like a countdown. Nico thought about his knee again. It hadn't hurt since he came across the creature. He flexed it experimentally, the old ache gone like smoke. He looked back at the creature and wondered what else it might be able to heal.

A short while later, the hum changed.

Nico was on the back porch, watching the rain loosen into mist, when it started. It was deeper now, edged with something sharp. Not the steady thrum in his skull he'd grown used to, but a pulse, like a searchlight sweeping for him. It made his teeth ache, the kind of vibration you felt more than heard. Even the porch boards under his boots seemed to buzz.

He rushed to the cellar to find the Vegetable Man standing on his own for the first time, head tilted toward the hills. Its body looked thinner than before, as if the air here was wearing it down. The lantern's glow slicked across its leaflike skin, highlighting veins that pulsed faintly, as though lit from within.

Through the crack in the cellar door, Nico caught movement between the trees—flashes of shadow where there shouldn't be any, quick bursts of pale light. And further off, the clumsy crash of boots through wet leaves.

"They're here," Nico said, but he didn't know exactly who "they" were. Were "they" whatever it was that hunted Vegetable Man on that other, strange world? Or were "they" more like Nico, in body if not in spirit?

The creature's gaze shifted past him. Toward the house.

Help, the creature's strange voice came into Nico's mind.

"I don't know how to help you," Nico said. "Other than hiding you."

The Vegetable Man shook its leafy head. *Help him,* it sent to Nico's mind.

With that, the creature brushed past Nico and went out of the cellar, headed for Saul's house. His long legs carried him so quickly across the yard and up onto the back porch that Nico had a hard time keeping up. Wet grass hissed under its feet, and Nico caught the sharp, electric scent of ozone trailing in its wake.

When they made it inside, they found Saul in his chair, mask hissing. He looked smaller than he had yesterday. The Vegetable Man bent toward him and laid a hand on his chest.

Nico felt it then, not in his head but in his bones. Another type of hum, one he realized he felt when he'd wiped the creature's blood on his pants leg, when his knee had started to feel better. It resonated through his ribcage, like standing too close to a church organ. The air in the room thickened, alive with static. The hairs on Nico's arms stood up.

Saul stirred, his breathing hitching, but then the creature pulled back. It shook its head, and Nico recognized a very human sadness in those very alien eyes.

Tried, it told Nico.

Saul must have heard it, too. He said, "I know you did. Now, you need to get out of here, before..."

From the woods, a shout. Too close.

Another followed, rough and commanding. Then the snap of branches under too many feet. Nico's pulse kicked hard. Whoever they were, they were nearly on top of them.

The Vegetable Man turned to Nico, and the sadness that had been in its eyes was now fear. It sent no words this time, just an image: Nico running downhill, light exploding between trees, the thing disappearing into dark water.

"I'll draw them off," Nico said, before it could ask.

He grabbed his jacket and ran back out to the cellar. He swiped his hands through the slick green blood on the cellar floor, smearing it across his sleeves. The smell was sharp, impossible to ignore. He was acting on instinct, somehow knowing that whatever was tracking the Vegetable Man was doing so because of its blood.

A moment later, the hum in his skull spiked. It was no longer background noise, but a piercing ache. He stumbled, pressing his fist to his temple, but forced himself to keep moving. If the hunters wanted a trail, he'd give them one.

Lights chased him through the trees, beams stabbing between trunks while voices called to one another. Behind them, something else moved, quieter but faster.

He had no idea if what was following him was human or not.

He cut downhill toward the cave mouth by the creek. He took off his jacket and tossed it into the cave before doubling back, carefully avoiding the hunters.

Shouts echoed as the beams converged on the cave mouth. He crouched low in the wet brush, heart hammering, and for a moment he thought he saw a shape not unlike the Vegetable Man itself—tall, angular, inhuman—flit through the light. But when the beams swung again, it was gone. Maybe just a shadow. Maybe not.

When he returned to Saul's property, the Vegetable Man was gone.

And it wasn't the only one.

The house was too quiet. Saul's mask still hissed steady in the half-light, but the man beneath it wasn't moving. Nico sat beside him, hand on the armrest, listening. The hum in his head had faded to almost nothing, just a faint echo of what it had been.

Just like Uncle Saul.

On the nightstand sat the folded clipping Saul had shown him, edges curling like it had been handled too many times. His uncle had been right about the creature. It wasn't dangerous. Just lost.

Nico touched the paper once, the ink flaking under his thumb. He thought of all the years Saul had carried the weight of a story no one believed. That was its own kind of exile: being pushed to the edge of your own town, your own family, because you dared to speak a truth that didn't fit their world.

Saul was buried at the edge of the property in an old family cemetery, where the woods pressed close. The ground was soft from days of rain.

Nico dug the grave with his hands as much as the shovel, earth caking under his nails, the smell of loam and rain heavy in his lungs. Birds gathered in the trees, restless witnesses to Nico's final act of love for the man who was more a father to him than his own dad. He wondered if the Vegetable Man was still out there, watching from some shadowed ridge, bearing witness in silence.

After, when cleaning out the cellar, Nico found something where the creature had lain while recovering. A seed, veined pale green, and still damp.

He turned it over in his palm. It pulsed faintly, like it had a heartbeat.

He planted it in the garden Saul had kept years ago, in a square of earth gone wild with weeds. He covered it over, patting the dirt flat.

That night, Nico dreamed. He dreamed of forests that weren't these, of skies with colors that didn't exist on Earth, of long-legged figures walking between trees without fear of hunters. He woke with tears on his face, though he couldn't have said why.

Weeks passed. The house stayed quiet, the papers on the desk gathering more dust. Nico drove to town sometimes for groceries, sometimes just to walk. The hum never came back, but neither did the soreness in his knee. He would catch himself testing it, half-expecting the old pain to return on the hills or the stairs. It never did. Some nights, lying awake, he thought he felt a phantom vibration in the floorboards. It was faint, as though something living still called faintly from beneath the soil.

Behind the house, in the softest corner of the garden, something new pushed through the soil. A thin green shoot, leaning toward the light.

It grew faster than it should have, curling upward with a purpose. Some mornings Nico thought he could almost hear it, the faintest vibration in the air, like the echo of that hum he'd carried in his skull for days. Not a burden now, but a promise.

Nico knelt, touched it gently. Its stem was warm under his fingers. It was alive, and reaching higher every day.

THE MOON WAS PALE..ISH

By Max Tackett

DEPENDIN' ON WHICH barn ya hang yer cognitive stock in, you might be one'a them folks that figgers there ain't no such thang as monsters. Maybe you believe what that slew'a Bible-thumpers 'cross the whole Tri-State's hollerin'—that if'n ya put yer faith in the Lord, all'll be well.

Or my personal favorite—you might just be sufferin' one'a them dee-loo-sional episodes, make ya wanna hole up in some bunker your daddy dug, chock-full'a canned beans and jugs'a piss water like the world's 'bout to up'n explode on itself. Funniest load'a shit I ever did hear, if'n ya ask me.

Point I'm tryin' to get 'cross is this—there's a mess-load'a shit folks put stock in. Most of it, far as I'm concerned, is just that. Shit.

Me? I never did put much trust in thangs I cain't see. Call me what ya want—realist, cynic, asshole—but I just don't go believin' in thangs that ain't stood in front'a me.

'At brings me to our current subject. Monsters. I, in fact, *do* believe in monsters. I don't believe in ghosts, or spirts, cain't see 'em. But, monsters, inn'a words of the great Randy Travis, "On the other hand," are real as kin be. They's real as a March rain, an' one night in Fallsburg, me an' my brother come 'cross the kind that walks 'neath the moon. Gimme a second will ya...

Ok, I refuse to do that any further. Have you *ever* tried to illustrate how we speak? It's terribly nerve wracking and nit-picky. The Southern Appalachia dialect is a standout for sure. But there's about ten other violent acts I would rather commit than to try and put those words to paper again.

By the way, the answer to your question is, yes. I, as a matter of fact, do indeed sound like the above individual. That's because I was raised in a small town in Kentucky named Louisa. Famous for the gas station the locals still refer to as "The Birdhouse." I can still taste the Baskin Robbins and smell the fumes from the American Electric Power plant right up the road on US 23. And if you keep driving past The Birdhouse, about seven and quarter miles, you'll arrive at my grandparents' house, in a little nook named Fallsburg. Which is where we begin.

There's a lot of memories in that house. For both myself, and my brother, who now owns the place. I remember being six years old and meeting my grandparents for the first time. Our Mom had remarried. The first thing I did was offer my grandfather one of those warhead sour candies. He did *not* partake, and I felt dumb.

Then there's the time, where, like an idiot, I decided to walk off the trail, literally, and got lost for about six hours. I think I was nine or ten. *Stop,* don't act like you've never ventured off in search of the *shiny* thing.

Finally, we come to the end of our introduction. We reach the memory where myself and my little brother, Bowen, were stalked and chased by what we now know as the "Moon Eyed People."

It's noteworthy to point out the geographical nature of the property in general. First off, the town of Fallsburg is *way* out in the sticks. It's cut off from the rest of the world. Like a bastard stepchild that you claim but hide from the rest. There's only one road in and one road out. Of course, that may have changed by now, but it's how I'll always remember it.

Winding roads with missing guard rails flanked by wild patches of ginseng on either side make for a scenic yet dangerous drive. You're sure to pass the "Mail Pouch" chewing tobacco barn on the left, that's how you know you're going in the right direction. Hills, creeks, the Big Sandy River, all accompanied by the sweet yet pungent stench of burning coal and oil.

The house itself is two stories, three if you count the basement, with paint peeling like fingernails in need of a manicure. The barn is red, and at one point it was bright red. But now, it shines with a shade that resembles raw pork. It remains a relic of the "good ol' days" and collects mold and whatever project our dad decides to undertake and then discard that week.

Then there's the field, where our story begins.

The following is a crucial detail, but it doesn't pertain *directly* to the story. I'll touch on this briefly because I don't wish to have the remainder of our experience overshadowed. My brother and I are both Marines; currently I'm almost at fifteen years, my brother did four and then decided to get out and pursue a career in construction. We both have multiple deployments, to various parts of the earth.

I only bring this up to reinforce that we both know what *is* and *what isn't*. I'm positive that if he and I reminisced with a thirty rack of mountain dew code red, we could likely generate at least two manuscripts worth of material. All surrounding the crazy shit we've seen.

We were on leave; it was 2021 and we both decided that we were going to head out to our grandparents' house in Fallsburg, to finally start putting the fence around the property. I think there's at least one hundred and fifty, to two hundred acres out there, maybe more. We had our work cut out for us, to say the least.

My brother, being the stud that he is, recently married and wanted to do a remodel of sorts on the house. Eventually, his long-term goal was to reside there full time. Livestock was never in question, as there was more than enough space to accommodate whatever breeds they desired.

He and I had just finished a late lunch and were headed back out to the field to continue working. I vividly remember being chilly—it was only about sixty degrees, but Kentucky gets to experience a real fall season, unlike the places on the coast where I routinely live. I didn't bring any layers with me, so I pulled on one of our dad's old Carhartt jackets.

It was only about two hundred yards from the porch to where we had started erecting the gate. We had our dog Binx with us—he was a pug and, in hindsight, more for morale support than anything. The little dude could only herd empty water bottles and, at the first sign of trouble, acted tough for less than a second before tucking tail and pulling a quick "bye, Felicia."

As we settled in and picked up where we had left off, I glanced up and saw the moon sliding out early—pale as old bone, watching us from the treeline.

We kept at it, digging posts and setting crossbeams, the kind of work that keeps your hands busy but leaves your mind wandering. Every so often, I'd glance back at the moon. It was stretching itself out, fattening into that full, round shape—bright enough you could almost fool yourself into thinking you didn't need lights at all. But the darker it got, the whiter it seemed to burn, like it was trying to lay claim to the whole sky.

We weren't in any hurry, so we just kept working. Bowen had us fixed up with contractor lights—tall metal stands with halogens that'll turn night into day if you aim them right. He was a project coordinator back then, so getting his hands on that kind of gear wasn't any trouble. They threw long yellow beams across the field, and the bugs came thick to dance in it, but just beyond the reach of that light was the kind of dark that feels like it's leaning in to listen.

It was maybe eight thirty when I noticed the first movement. At the far edge of the light, just where the trees started, two pale shapes stood side by side. At first, I thought they were fence posts catching the moon—until they shifted.

I nudged Bowen with my elbow. "See that?"

He turned, eyes narrowing. "Yeah." He raised his voice. "Hey! You lost?"

The figures didn't move.

"You need a hand?" I called.

Silence. Then a cloud slid across the moon, dimming the whole field. When it cleared, they were gone.

We went back to work, both of us stealing glances at the treeline. Around nine o'clock, they showed again. Closer this time—maybe thirty yards out. I could tell now they weren't wearing anything that made sense for the weather. Bare arms, bare legs, pale like the inside of a shell.

Bowen stepped toward them until the shadows of the lights stretched long across the grass. "You need directions?" It wasn't uncommon for people to go wandering and get lost on someone else's property.

Nothing. No movement, no talking. Just... watching.

I remembered something our grandmother used to say about the hills around Fallsburg. Sitting on her porch, she'd tell us about the old caves in the area—some natural, some mine shafts from a century back. "There's holes under these hills lead clear to places you don't wanna go," she'd say. "Dark places make dark things." I'd always thought she meant wild animals, maybe folks hiding out. Now I wasn't so sure.

Another cloud rolled across the moonlight. By the time it passed, the shapes were gone again.

We took a short break, sat on the tailgate, drinking water. The lights hummed. Binx gave a short, sharp bark toward the trees and then went quiet, just watching.

At about nine thirty, I went to grab another post and froze. They were back—ten yards closer than before, just inside the edge of the light. This time I could see faces. Smooth, pale, no hair I could make out, and eyes that caught the moonlight in a way that made them look like wet silver.

Bowen walked up beside me. "Alright," he called, his voice firm now, "if you need something, you can say so."

I added, "It's gettin' late. If you're lost, we can get you somewhere warm."

They didn't move. Didn't blink. Just stood there like the idea of answering didn't apply to them.

The hair on my arms stood up. The air felt wrong—heavier, cooler. Another cloud passed over the moon. When the light returned, the edge of the field was empty again.

We decided to finish the section we were working on and be done for the night. At ten sharp, we killed the tools and started loading the truck.

When I shut off the contractor lights, the moon took over, throwing silver across the grass and turning the treeline into a perfect black cutout. And there—farther back now, half-hidden between the trunks—were the same pale shapes. Watching.

Neither of us said a word. We just gathered the last of the tools, Binx at our heels, and started back toward the house.

Madison was still up when we came in, leaning against the kitchen counter with her phone in one hand and a mug of tea in the other.

"You two look like you seen a ghost," she said.

Bowen dropped his gloves on the table and shook his head. "Not a ghost. People."

I set my Carhartt on the chair. "Not people like you mean."

We told her everything. The first sighting way out by the treeline, the second one closer, and the third one where we saw their faces—pale, smooth, and those strange moon-silver eyes that didn't reflect the halogen lights.

"You sure it wasn't just kids screwin' around?" she asked.

"Kids?" Bowen leaned forward on the table. "In bare skin, in sixty degree weather, in the middle of the woods, not sayin' a damn word? And disappearin' every time a cloud covers the moon?"

Madison glanced toward the dark kitchen window, then back at us. "That's... weird."

We headed upstairs a little after ten thirty, but I stopped at the landing window, the one that overlooked the field. Habit, I guess. I wanted to see the fence line we'd worked on.

And there they were.

Not at the treeline this time. Out in the open. Standing in the moonlight where the grass rolled down from the barn toward the fence.

There were more of them now—five, maybe six. They weren't huddled together, just spread out like they'd been there all along, waiting for us to notice.

I froze. "Bowen."

He stepped up beside me, saw where I was looking, and hissed a quiet "Shit."

The moonlight left no shadows to hide in. I could see them clearly now. Short—maybe five feet at most—but with long limbs that didn't seem to match their bodies. Skin pale enough to almost glow. No hair. Faces... wrong. Not deformed exactly, but too smooth. The eyes were the worst—large, pale, reflective like a cat's, but flat and unblinking.

One of them tilted its head, slow and bird-like, and I felt something in my stomach knot tight.

Madison came up behind us. "What is it?"

Neither of us answered right away. Finally, Bowen said, "Look for yourself."

She did—and to her credit, she didn't scream. She just gripped the windowsill until her knuckles went white. "What the hell..."

We watched them for maybe thirty seconds. They didn't move closer. Didn't wave. Didn't run. Just stood there, each one turned toward the house like they'd been caught mid-approach.

Then, as if some signal passed between them, they began to move— slow, deliberate steps backward toward the treeline. Not turning around, just walking backward, eyes locked on us.

When the moon went behind a cloud, they vanished.

We didn't stay upstairs long. Bowen said, "We can't just sit here wondering."

Dad's house had no shortage of guns. Behind the laundry room door, propped neatly in the corner, were two of his favorites: a .30-30 lever-action and a twelve-gauge pump. Both clean, both loaded.

Bowen took the shotgun. I grabbed the rifle. We each checked the chamber and pocketed a handful of extra shells. The smell of gun oil filled the narrow hallway, familiar and grounding.

"Madison, you stay here," Bowen said.

"And if you see something?" she asked.

"Then we know," I told her.

Outside, the night was sharp and damp. The moon hung high, silvering every blade of grass. We moved past the barn, our boots whispering against the ground, flashlights sweeping slow arcs.

They stepped out from the far side of the fence, one at a time, until there were six again. Pale, long-limbed, heads cocked slightly as they studied us.

Up close, the skin was almost translucent, with faint blue veins. Faces shallow-featured, no hair, no eyebrows. The eyes caught the moon and our lights, reflecting back a cold, metallic silver.

"Hey!" Bowen called, shotgun steady. "You're on private property. You need to turn around."

No response.

They began to move forward.

We backed toward the barn. The smell hit me—damp stone and something metallic, like blood on cold iron.

The closest one's mouth opened, showing small, uniform teeth—too perfect to be natural, almost like they'd been made in a mold. The rest mirrored it, jaws parting in eerie unison. No sound. No hiss, no breath, no click of teeth. Just... open.

Every part of me wanted to take a step back, but my boots felt locked to the ground. My thumb itched over the rifle's safety, the weight of the stock pressing firm into my shoulder. I knew that if one of them even twitched toward me, I'd squeeze the trigger without a second thought.

Bowen's voice cut through the stillness—low but hard. "That's far enough."

It should have been enough. Most things in these parts, human or animal, understand that tone. But they didn't flinch. Didn't even blink.

They kept walking.

Slow steps, the kind that don't kick up grass or make the dirt shift. They didn't sway or stumble, just... glided forward like they knew every inch of the ground between us and them.

By now they were close enough for me to see more than just those pale faces. Their skin wasn't just white—it was thin. Veins branched under it like faded river maps. No muscle definition I could see, but there was a strange stillness in the way they held themselves, as if they didn't need muscle. Their shoulders hung low, arms swinging just enough to keep balance.

The smell hit me next. Damp stone, like the inside of an old well. Underneath it, faint but sharp, was something metallic—like the tang of blood on a rusted knife.

I swallowed hard. My tongue felt dry, my mouth clamped shut so tight it hurt. Bowen's shotgun shifted slightly, the beam from our flashlights catching the lead figure full in the face.

That's when it tilted its head. Not like a curious dog—slower, sharper, the way a predator measures distance.

My mind flashed back to something Grandma had said once when I was maybe ten, about the caves up in the hills. She'd been snapping beans on the porch, and I'd been bored, staring off toward the ridge. She told me, "Some things don't like the light, but they sure as hell know how to move in it when they want to." I'd asked her what she meant, and she just said, "Dark places make dark things, Maxie. If you see somethin' that's too still, that's your sign to move along."

Now I understood what she meant.

They didn't stop until we stepped into the barn's shadow. I don't know if it was deliberate or coincidence, but the moment the moonlight left my boots, every single one of them froze. It was like someone had hit a pause button on a movie.

We stood there in a silence so thick I could hear my own heartbeat in my ears. My forearms ached from the tension of holding the rifle so steady. I wanted to glance at Bowen, but I didn't dare take my eyes off them.

One of them—not the lead, but one just off to the right—shifted its weight slightly. The grass beneath its bare foot didn't even bend. That's when I realized they weren't breathing.

A long moment passed. My flashlight beam wavered slightly, and in that small movement, I noticed something—their eyes didn't reflect like an animal's. The silver wasn't a reflection at all. It was coming from *inside*.

Then, in perfect unison, they turned. Not pivoting like a person would, but as if their whole bodies were on a swivel.

They walked back toward the trees, still facing us, never breaking eye contact. Step after slow step, they closed the distance to the treeline without once looking behind them.

The moon went behind a cloud.

For a few seconds, everything was darkness except the narrow cones of our flashlights. I swept mine over the treeline, over the grass, over the fence posts. Nothing. Just empty space where they'd been seconds before.

When the moonlight came back, the field was empty.

We didn't move right away. Bowen was the first to take a step back toward the house, keeping his shotgun shouldered until we were halfway to the porch. Only when the boards creaked under our boots did he lower it.

Inside, Madison was waiting at the kitchen window, her hands braced on the sink like she'd been glued there the whole time we were gone.

"Well?" she asked, eyes flicking from my face to Bowen's.

"They're gone," Bowen said, leaning the shotgun against the wall but not letting go of it completely.

"For now," I added. I knew it in my bones—we hadn't scared them off. They'd left because they wanted to, and they could come back any damn time.

Madison tried to brush it off at first, saying maybe it was just trespassers trying to spook us. But when Bowen told her exactly how close they'd gotten—how we could see the veins under their skin, the uniform teeth, the way they moved in unison—she stopped talking.

"You think they're... people?" she asked finally.

"No," Bowen said, shaking his head. "I think they're somethin' else."

I went to the window and looked out again. The field was still. The contractor lights were off now, so the moon was doing all the work. Every fence post stood in a silver halo, the barn's shadow stretching across the grass like a scar.

Madison came up beside me, speaking quieter now. "So what do we do?"

"Lock the doors," I said. "Keep the lights low. Don't give 'em reason to come closer."

We spent the next half hour doing exactly that—checking each door, making sure every window was latched. Madison closed the blinds in the living room, but I left a small gap in the kitchen curtain so I could keep an eye on the field.

At one point, Binx started growling low from under the table. His eyes were fixed on the back door. I flicked off the kitchen light and peered out.

There was nothing there. No movement in the yard. No shapes in the grass. But I swear the dark felt thicker in that direction, like the night itself was leaning closer.

When I turned the light back on, Binx had already retreated to the corner, still growling under his breath.

It was after midnight before we even tried to go upstairs. Madison went first, Bowen behind her, me last with the rifle in my hands. I told myself I'd set it down once we were settled, but I didn't.

In my old room, I sat on the edge of the bed, boots still on, watching the slice of moonlight on the floor from the window. The house was quiet except for the occasional creak of old wood. I could hear Bowen in the room across the hall, pacing slow, the floorboards giving him away.

Every so often, I thought I heard something outside—not loud, just a faint shifting, like someone dragging a foot through the grass.

Around one, I gave in and went to the landing window again. The field was empty. The moon was high and sharp, the kind that makes every shadow look deeper.

I told myself they were gone for the night. I told myself we'd wake up in the morning, finish the fence, and never see them again. But deep down, I knew better.

Because if there's one thing Grandma was right about, it's this:

Dark places make dark things. And sometimes, they come out to see who's been working in their light.

THE PRIVY DIG

By Michael Fitzgerald

ADDIE SLOWED HER digging with the trowel and switched over to the hog-hair brush. She didn't want to risk damaging any discoveries. After a few passes with the sturdy bristles, a shiny surface was revealed. This wasn't another rock, but something that had been placed down there. She stood up, her head just peering over the top of the edge of the pit.

"I found something!"

Nathan, the dig leader of WVU's Cultural Heritage Studies Program, grabbed his camera from its bag and ran over. Constance and Ian, who were enjoying a cup of coffee and reviewing land maps, put their mugs on the hood of the Land Cruiser and went to check the find, which would be the first at this location; the yard behind a 1920s farmhouse in Point Pleasant, WV that was still in use.

Addie switched over to a toothbrush and slowly worked the side of the object, revealing raised text. The others were now standing on the edge of the pit, a hole cut in the ground four feet in diameter and almost five feet deep.

"Can you make anything out?" Constance asked. "What color is it?" She opened a leather journal and took notes.

"It's blue glass. Dark blue. The letters I see so far are 'OMO', Dash, 'SEL' in all caps."

"I'll take a few more shots and then try to pull it out," Nathan said. He placed a small basket at the edge of the pit. Inside was a white cotton cloth covering the bottom.

Estimating the size and shape of the object, Addie used the trowel to score indentations, listening for any contact as she pushed into the night soil. She pressed her fingers around the sides of the prize and pulled it loose. It was covered with several inches of caked dirt. She reached up and placed it into the basket.

Ian gave her a hand out of the pit and they walked over to the makeshift inspection station, which was comprised of a folding table with a plastic tub, several brushes and dental picks, towels, and a container of water. Nathan picked up the basket and went to the inspection station. He first broke as much loose dirt away from the object as possible, letting it fall into the basket. They could go through the cloth later to make certain no other parts were missed. He then placed it in the tub and poured water over it. He washed it with a brush and used the dental pick to get the last remnants of soil out of the lettering. After drying it with a towel, he held up a dark blue 4" tall by 1-1/2" wide bottle.

"What Ms. French has found is a perfect specimen of an Emerson Drug Bromo-Seltzer bottle," Nathan proclaimed.

Addie took a picture of him with her phone. They cheered.

"Not bad for six hours' work," Nathan said. "Let's put it with the other eight bottles we've collected this week. Besides the Bromo-Seltzer, we've found bitters and stool softener."

"The people of these parts did not eat well," Addie said.

"I wish we had something more substantial. There's nothing exhibition quality in there," Nathan said. "I know this is important information. It's a snapshot of how people lived. The limited choices they had. I just think this study needs something more."

"Who would have thought that we'd be digging in a toilet to learn the past?"

"Trust me. My parents get a kick out of explaining to their friends what I do," Addie said, digging dirt from under her nails with a metal file. "I know it's decades old and just compost at this point, but it feels different from regular dirt. It seems damper and colder."

"It's in your head, Addie," Ian said.

She held up her hands. "It's in my skin. It's under my nails. It gets everywhere."

"Who's next?" Nathan asked.

Constance raised her hand. "I'm ready for the pit, sir."

Nathan pointed to the dig site. "Send her to the pit!"

Ian and Addie helped her into the hole, and she continued excavating the site. Addie washed her hands, brushed the dirt from her jeans, and poured a cup of lukewarm coffee. She looked at the farmhouse that sat 50 yards away, trying to imagine the walk they had from the back door to this spot several times a day before the modern septic system was installed. Having to trudge out here in bad weather, in the freezing cold and while ill must have been miserable. It made her appreciate the luxuries she was afforded in her much more comfortable life as an instructor at the university. She knew having her name on this study would help secure her tenure at the university.

By the end of the afternoon, they'd recovered several small medicine bottles, some loose change dating back to 1910, a broken China coffee cup and a partial set of dentures. Ian filled the hole. They always left the site as they found it. As Addie and Constance packed the gear, Nathan thanked the owners of the property for the use and showed them the haul. He explained how the items would be used in their studies and where they would be on display as part of the growing collection of cultural artifacts found in this area.

Ian studied the map for a quicker route to get them off the rural road that seemed to wind and twist endlessly. The woods continued on as far as he could see, making Nathan nervous that he was headed in the wrong direction. The afternoon sun darted in and out from between the trees.

"We've had better hauls," Constance said, reviewing her journal. "How does one lose their dentures?"

"Maybe they took them out to clean them and lost their grip," Nathan offered. "Or they fell out when they were tossing the cookies, as noted by all the stomach meds we found."

"And once your teeth go into the privy, they are gone," Addie laughed.

"They always said granny's got a shit eatin' grin," Ian said.

"Oh," Nathan groaned. "Not good, Ian. Not good."

Addie leaned up from the back seat. "So, where are we?"

Ian huffed. "We should be coming up to 35. That gets us off this back road, and eventually out to the interstate."

Constance tapped on the window. "Hey, did you all see that?"

"What's that, Connie?" Ian asked, lowering the map.

"It looked like a farmhouse, just off the side of the road. I haven't seen a house in a while."

Nathan slowed to a stop. He turned in the seat and looked out the back of the Land Cruiser. "I don't see anything."

Ian rolled down his window and poked his head out. "You sure?"

"It was set back, not too far. Looked much older than the last place."

"We'll take a quick look," Nathan said. "A minute won't throw us off schedule." He put the truck in reverse and backed down the road.

"I still don't see anything," Ian said.

As they backed, the silhouette of a house emerged through tall grass and brush, a short distance from the road. Nathan stopped in front of the house.

"Good eye, Connie," Nathan said. "If I were going any faster, we would have missed it."

"I don't think anyone's been there in years," Addie said, leaning over Constance to look out the side window.

"How do we get there?" Nathan asked.

"Seriously?" Ian asked.

"Why else would we have stopped?" Nathan said. "Let's at least look. Is there a driveway?"

"I think there's a clearing behind us," Constance said.

Nathan reversed and stopped at a section of brush that was much thinner and shorter than the rest. The side of the house was more visible from this angle. "I believe we found the driveway."

He drove slowly along the path. Brush rubbed the sides and undercarriage of the truck. They swayed as they entered ruts in the worn road. After fifty feet, the brush thinned, and they had a clear view of the house. It was a two-story farmhouse, dilapidated and abandoned. The windows that weren't broken were missing. There was no paint left on the house, leaving it a dingy gray. Part of the overhang of the front porch had collapsed and there was a hole in the roof.

"I'm liking it!" Nathan said.

"This has to be the oldest house out here," Ian said.

"Wait, you guys don't want to check out this place?" Addie asked.

"I hate to go back with what little we have on hand," Nathan explained. "The age of this house might give us some older findings. What we've found so far doesn't lend itself to a good representation of life out here. The assortment we have is seriously lacking. I'd like to go further back in history. This house could help fill in a few gaps in our paper."

Nathan continued through the grass and pulled in behind the house on a short gravel strip. He got out and waved for the others to follow. He took several photos of the layout. Constance got out and walked up to Nathan. She covered her eyes from the noonday sun and scanned the grounds. The others joined them.

"Without the owners here, how easily do you think you'll be able to locate the outhouse?" Constance asked. "And how many did they have? You're looking for the original, not the most recent one."

"That's true," Nathan said. "But Ian has an eye for these things. Don't you?"

Ian winked. "You betcha." He walked to the back of the Land Cruiser and opened the hatch. He removed a long metal rod with a hollow tube cross handle. They followed him to the back of the house.

"First," Ian explained, "we look for a path made from years of people walking to the outhouse. They usually built them out to the corners of the house, several yards away. We also look for apple trees or lilac bushes. The owners would plant them to help mask the smell." He pointed and laughed. "I don't believe it."

Off to the left was a large apple tree. Its bark was thick, scaly and peeling. The only fruits on the tree were small, diseased, and covered with insects. There were many twisty branches, mostly bare. Ian walked up to the tree.

"This masked the smell of an outhouse?" Addie giggled.

Ian tapped a dried fruit with the privy probe. "It's been neglected for decades. It was probably full of apples in its day."

Constance waved her hands out in front of her. "So, Sherlock, where is it?"

Nathan and Addie began chanting, "Ian! Ian!"

Constance joined in.

Ian spun around, examining the grounds. He looked at the house, followed a small rise back toward it, spun around and took several steps to his left, now standing in waist high switch grass. Ian raised the probe and drove it into the ground.

"Now's the test," he smiled.

Applying pressure and a twisting motion, he pushed the probe into the ground. It continued slowly going down. He laughed. "That's right, keep going. Sweet, sweet night soil."

"Never doubted you," Nathan said, turning to the truck. He opened the back and slid out a shovel.

"Such a poetic term for human manure," Constance noted.

Ian continued pushing the probe, holding onto the hollow handle with both hands. He shook his head as he pressed it downward. When the probe got halfway in, he stopped.

"Something?" Nathan asked.

Ian nodded. He pulled upward slightly, smiling, and then pressed back downward. "We got something."

"Stand where you are, Ian," Nathan said. "I want to get a few shots before you break ground." He took photos of Ian holding the probe, of the location of the dig site and of the back of the house. "Addie, would you mind nosing around the outside of the house to see if there's any family info? Any name plaques, old license plates or even newspapers that could give us information for the report?"

Addie grabbed a cloth sack from the car and walked to the house. Constance helped Nathan set up the inspection station while Ian began digging.

Ian pressed the probe into the earth several more times to outline a safe area around the item to extract. He switched over to a shovel and scooped out a section of dirt with the embedded object. This was placed on a tarp beside the dig site for the others to slowly sift through so as not to destroy any artifacts. Ian went back to probing as Addie and Constance worked on the sample.

"I think it's metal," Addie said as she separated the dirt with a trowel. "I felt it scrape against the blade."

Constance ran a hog-hair brush across the object as it protruded from the lump of dirt. "Oh my," she said. "Nathan, you might want to take over here."

"Is there a problem?"

"I think it's a gun."

Nathan went over to the tarp and knelt down. He took a bottle of water and poured it over the side of the object, revealing a cylinder and part of the handle. "Yep, someone chucked a gun in the shitter."

"It's more common than you think," Ian said, leaning on the probe. "You find granddad's worn old piece after he dies and need to get rid of it."

"Or you carried it out with you in case you ran into snakes or other wildlife, and it just falls in," Nathan added.

"Cause once it falls into the privy," Addie laughed.

"It's gone," Constance finished.

"Let me check that it's empty before we bag and transport it," Nathan said. "I'll have to record the serial number and report it, but we'll get to keep it with the collection."

"Probably," Ian said.

They looked at him.

"Hey, you never know what happened here," he said. "We don't know why no one lives here. Could have history." He straightened up, grabbed the probe and jammed it into the ground again.

Nathan held the gun in his fingers at the handle, aiming it at the ground. Using a toothbrush, he cleaned the soil from around the cylinder. "Most likely fell out of someone's pocket while they were using the toilet." He poured water on the gun and inspected it. "I see shells, but don't know if they're spent." He pressed on the cylinder release and it slid out the side. The shells fell onto the tarp when he pushed the ejector slide. "They're spent, and the gun is safe. Let's bag it. Nice find, Ian."

Addie dropped a specimen bag on the tarp. "I don't want to handle that. I don't like guns."

Nathan wiped the water from the gun with a cloth and dropped the gun into the bag. Constance had been filling out a label. She handed it to Ian, and he stuck it on the bag.

"Hey, guys, I think I got something else," Ian said.

"Could be shells for the gun," Nathan said.

"No, it's not metal. It's not giving me that metal grind."

"Just a loose rock from the side walls?" Constance asked.

"No, it's not like rock. Bit odd. Let me trace the outline." Ian again outlined the perimeter of the object with the probe. This time, the area was much larger. "We might have a group of items here. I can't imagine it's this large. I'm going to have to be careful getting this out."

Ian cut out a two-foot section of ground. Nathan put his gloves back on, jumped into the hole, and they slid their fingers around the mass of dirt. They hefted the ball up and out onto the tarp. Nathan hopped out of the shallow hole, helped Ian up, and they rolled the clump to the center of the tarp. Addie snapped several shots of the curious mound.

"Go at it," Nathan said.

Addie and Constance knelt in front of the small mound and chiseled away from the edges with trowels. Ian went back to the dig and continued probing. Addie's tool struck something solid. She slowed, followed its contour, and scooped a section of material away.

"I've got something here," she said. "I think it's bone."

Nathan pulled out a pocketknife and scraped a length of the exposed section with the back of the blade so as to not damage it. "I believe you're right. That's bone. Be careful now. Go slowly."

She continued, exposing more of the specimen. It quickly became apparent it was a skull. Addie dropped her tool, stood and stepped back. "I'm done," she said. "If that's an infant, I'll lose it."

"That's fine, Addie," Nathan said. "You don't have to do anything you don't want to." He turned to Constance. "You have a biology background. Do you mind?"

She made a sighing sound. "I'm not saying I won't freak out as well. But I'll take a look." She knelt down and slowly exposed more of the skull. When she got to the jaw, it extended too much forward to be human and had two large canine teeth. "Not an infant," she announced.

"Thank god," Addie said.

"Well, not a human infant," Constance added, as she worked. "See the sagittal suture here?" She pointed to a wavy line across the top of the skull with the handle of the tool. "It's not fused. And the thinness of the bone. It's very delicate for an animal this size. I'm going to say it was relatively young."

Nathan leaned over and took a picture of the skull. "Is it a dog? Maybe a wolf? They used to inhabit these hills."

"This has a large, square nasal opening. And the eye sockets are also much larger than a canine's," she noted. "I think it's a bear cub."

"Aww, why would they put a bear cub in there?" Addie moaned. "They're so cute."

"But the mama isn't so cute," Nathan said.

"She's very protective and aggressive," Constance said. "Look here." She highlighted a newly exposed hole in the back of the skull. "Someone might have killed it and dumped it to stop mama from coming around."

"I might be even more bummed," Addie said.

"Well, that is a most interesting find," Nathan said. "At best, we're lucky to find empty bottles of ancient abortifacient or a stash of opium-laced cough medicines. Those can offer an interesting narrative to what is typically a sterile, academic report. But I must say, this is new and will make quite the yarn. Great job. Let's clean that up and wrap it. We'll call it a day."

Addie knelt back down and began carving dirt away from the find. Constance looked over at her.

"I might be bummed about it, but if it means we get out of here early, I'm ready to help."

"I'll give the dig site a few more probes while they finish up," Ian said. "Never know."

Nathan pulled a large plastic container out of the truck and placed it next to the tarp. "We'll pack the parts of the specimen in here."

Constance removed the skull from the section of dirt and used a sturdy brush to clean it. She slowly turned the skull several times, examining it. "This has strange protrusions on it. They seem to be made of bone. Look at the back of the skull. It should be smooth here, but there's a mix of spikes and what looks like a small horn. Some type of deformity."

"Poor guy," Addie said, as she revealed an arm and portion of the shoulder. "Maybe its mother abandoned it?"

"Right after birth, I don't doubt," Constance said. "Can you imagine how bad that thing must have hurt coming out?"

"Oh, my god!" Addie yelped. "Check out this arm. It's covered with those spikes and there's some type of flat sections of bone jutting out."

"May I?" Nathan asked, kneeling next to the skeleton. He brushed the arm clean down to the paw. On it were long, extended claws. "Holy crap! Look at those things."

"Maybe they did mama a favor," Ian said, now out of the hole packing the probe in the back of the truck.

"Mama could have been worse," Constance said. "These genetic defects could have run in the family."

"Well, this story keeps getting more interesting," Nathan said. "Let's get this cleaned and boxed."

They worked together and removed the bones from the night soil, placed them in sections of cloth, then into the tub, and finally placed them in the rear of the vehicle. Ian filled the hole, leaving the grounds as close to how they originally found it as he could. They packed the rest of the gear, cleaned up and got into the Land Cruiser.

"I feel much better about these last two days now," Nathan said. "After we get back and finish the report and present our findings, I think the school will be pleased with our excursion. It will be a project you should be proud of." He started the truck, got ready to pull out, then noticed a light on the dash. "Damn, I think I've got a low tire. Hold on." Nathan reached over and pulled a digital tire gauge from the glove box.

"Oh, I can't believe this," Addie said.

Nathan checked the front driver's side tire, stood up, and nodded. "Yep, it's low." He poked his head into the cab. "Don't worry, I carry a portable inflator. Should only take a sec." He walked to the rear of the vehicle and paused. He bent over and checked the rear tire. "Shit!"

"What's wrong?" Ian yelled.

"It's low too."

"Oh, no! Stop with that," Addie said.

Everyone was getting out.

"Let me guess?" Constance said.

Nathan opened the rear hatch and pulled out the inflator. He hooked it to the dash and the front driver's side tire. Ian walked behind the Land Cruiser on the path they drove in on. Addie pulled a vape from her pocket and took a deep hit, then offered it to Constance.

The inflator made a loud humming noise and danced on the ground as it filled the tire. Ian stopped at the edge of the wall of weeds that covered the path in.

"Hey, you all, come here," he shouted. "But keep a lookout."

The women ran toward Ian. Nathan shut off the inflator and joined them.

"Keep a lookout for what?" Constance asked.

Ian separated the tall weeds with his foot. "This!"

Hidden in the weeds were several boards with long nails sticking out of them.

"Who in the hell?" Nathan mumbled.

"What do you think the purpose of this was?" Ian asked.

Nathan lifted up one of the boards. It had "DANGER – DO NOT ENTER!" in red paint scrawled across the board. "Shit! I think I drove over the warning sign that was hidden by the tall grass."

"You couldn't fill the tire?" Constance asked.

"No go," Nathan said.

"What are we going to do?" Addie panicked.

Nathan pulled out his phone. "Believe it or not, I've got service. Let's see if I can get someone out here. Ian, find a clear path around that. Make sure there's no more surprises. Something near the house."

Ian went to the truck and grabbed the probe, then walked a path between the truck and the house. He swiped the probe in the grass as he walked. "Connie, can you find some long sticks or branches so I can mark the path?" he asked her.

She and Addie went off to locate some sticks. Nathan came back and caught up with Ian, who was standing waist deep in weeds.

"All is not lost. There's a garage that's sending a wrecker out here," he said. "I've given them my GPS."

Addie dumped a few sticks at the edge of the tall grass. "How long?"

"Might be a few hours," Nathan said, glancing at his watch. "Let's hang on the porch until they arrive." He picked up a few limbs from the ground and handed them to Ian. "Think you got a clear path for the wrecker?"

"If they follow these sticks, they'll be safe," he said. "I'll be able to guide them."

Nathan leaned in. "Bring a few of those sticks and we'll make a fire out front. It'll help signal the wrecker in case it gets dark before they arrive."

Ian looked at his watch. "Could be tight. I'll find some rocks and make a proper fire ring. It's been a while. I miss the old camp counselor days."

"Please put off the campfire songs until absolutely necessary." Nathan walked to the truck. "You all might want to grab a snack or a drink and then meet me in front of the house."

Ian used a mix of large stones and old bricks to build a fire ring. There was enough dry brush and sticks to quickly have a fire going, with the help of a disposable lighter. Constance and Addie sat on the front steps on the porch, digging through a bag of fruit and energy bars.

"So how long are we really going to wait, Nathan?" Addie asked, gnawing on chocolate-covered granola.

"They should be here shortly," Nathan said.

"If it gets any later," Constance said, "they might miss the campfire."

"It's not that late, Connie," Nathan reassured. "I'll call and check on the wrecker."

"Did you hear that?" Ian asked. He put his hand up to quiet the group.

"What's up?" Nathan whispered.

"I thought I heard movement out back. Something rustling in the brush."

Addie picked up a stick next to the campfire. "I've dealt with plenty of raccoons messing with our garbage back home. I'll show them who's boss. We don't need anything messing with the cruiser."

"Alright, Conan," Nathan said, holding her back. "I appreciate the enthusiasm, but let's do this right."

From behind the house came a loud metallic crash, like a refrigerator had been dropped from the roof. Everyone else reached down and picked up a stick.

"What the hell was that?" Ian said. "Was that the cruiser?"

Staying near the side of the house, the group slowly ventured around to the back. As they rounded the corner of the house, they saw the Land

Cruiser on its roof, rear hatch open and the contents spilled across the ground.

"It's not raccoons," Constance whispered.

"You see anything?" Nathan asked Ian.

"I can't see anything farther than the dig site. I forgot how quickly it gets dark out here. I wish that gun we found still worked."

"That's got to be mama or a sibling, something real freakin' big," Addie said.

"Want to get inside the house?" Ian asked.

"Yeah, that's a good idea," Nathan said. "Let me get the flashlight from the glove box. That's if the door will open."

"You can't go out there," Constance said, pulling on his shirt.

Nathan pointed to the storage container that held the skeleton. It was torn to shreds and empty, lying among the rest of their supplies. "It's gone. It got what it came for. I'll be quick."

He darted out, staying low to the front of the truck, stick ready in hand. He pointed to his eyes, then to the group, asking if they saw anything. They all shook their heads. Nathan crept around the front to the side of the truck when he noticed that the nose of the vehicle was slowly rising. He stood to match the height of the front end. As it kept rising, he took several steps back, away from it. The nose swung back down, smashing the hood to the ground. Towering over the rear of the Land Cruiser was an eight-foot monstrosity, its paws on the bottom of the vehicle, rocking it like a child's toy.

"Run, Nathan! Run!" Addie screamed.

The beast had spiked bone protrusions jutting from its face and body. Horns of different sizes extended from its head in awkward angles. It had mottled and patchy fur, scarred from years of fighting. Its paws were the size of frying pans, with claws like daggers.

Nathan took a few more steps back, and the horror roared. Spittle flew from its enormous mouth. It swung a paw down and its claw ripped into a tire that blew apart, sending strips of rubber and nylon banding across the brush. Nathan froze in terror. He could smell its breath from across the truck. It smelled like hot death.

Suddenly, the beast was engulfed in high-powered lights. Racing up the path was a wrecker, with its spotlights ablaze. The creature reared back, using its paws to block the light. It roared. The wrecker blasted its air horn, sounding as though it belonged on a locomotive. Shingles on the house reverberated.

"Get in!" the driver yelled.

He opened his door, stepped out on the running board, and flipped the seat forward. They ran to the wrecker and piled in. Nathan ran to the passenger side. Before he could shut the door, the wrecker was in reverse and backing out at full speed, removing a section of the fence as it cut wildly onto the road.

"If you need anything from back there," the driver said, "you're on your own. I ain't comin' back."

Nathan checked the back seat to make sure everyone had made it safely.

"I think we're good," Nathan said. "Keep driving."

"What in the hell was that?" Ian asked.

"I picked up a car from around here many years ago with its top ripped off like a sardine can," the wrecker driver said. "An old timer from the shop went on about a Bone Bear in these parts. That's not what I was expecting."

"So, does this go into your study?" Constance asked. "You wanted an interesting story."

"Right now, without any proof of our finds, I'm not sure we even have a study. Just another tall tale," Nathan said. "I don't want to be that crackpot professor who keeps telling the story about the monstrosity he faced while in the field." He turned to the back seat. "Do you?"

They shook their heads. Constance took a hit on her vape.

Nathan sat back in the seat. "In some ways, that pit was a grave for that pitiful thing. You could almost understand why desecrating it would have pissed off its mother." He stared out the greasy windshield of the tow truck. "What we call archaeology, others may view as defilement. We should learn to respect our boundaries."

THE NOT DEER

By S.E. Howard

THROUGH THE WINDOW, just beyond the smudge of film caused by his breath against the glass, Gabe Myer caught sight of a deer. It stood past the edge of dense woods beside the narrow gravel road along which the SUV jostled. It appeared to be a buck, but although his glimpse was too fleeting to count the number of points on its rack as they drove past, Gabe saw the deer long enough to realize there was something off about it.

Maybe it was because it didn't shy away from the sight of the truck, the rumble of its engine, or the loose grit rattling noisily as it bounced and ricocheted off the underside. Or maybe it was the way the buck simply stood there, shrouded in shadows, its gaze fixed with unerring focus as they drove by.

That's weird, Gabe thought.

"Oh, wow." Mom hadn't noticed the deer at all, her attention turned instead toward the two-story log house they approached. "Is that it?"

"I think so," Louis replied. "It looks like the pictures from the website."

"It's beautiful," Mom said. "Don't you think, Gabe?"

She really wanted it to be a good thing, this getaway near the Nantahala National Forest in North Carolina, in the heart of the Appalachian Mountains. Personally, Gabe would have rather gone to a beach somewhere, or a theme park down in Florida. Universal Orlando might have made spending time with Louis seem tolerable.

"Uh, yeah," he said. He turned in his seat to look through the rear windshield, but the buck was no longer visible. "It's great."

As Louis slowed the SUV to a stop at the end of the driveway, they saw a dusty pickup truck already parked there and waiting. The driver's side door opened and an old man stepped out, lifting his hand in a wave.

"Is that the owner?" Mom asked.

"Must be." Louis cut the ignition and turned to her with a smile. "Let's go say hello."

When Gabe pushed his door open, a wall of humidity immediately engulfed him. Squinting against the glare of the midafternoon sun, feeling the back of his t-shirt already wanting to stick to the skin between his shoulder blades with a fresh bloom of sweat, he looked back at the line of trees abutting the road. There was no sign of the deer.

"Mr. Farnsdale?" Louis asked, offering his hand. "Louis Bradshaw. We spoke on the phone."

The old man wiped his palm against the leg of his denim biballs before accepting the clasp. "Pleasure's all mine," he said, his voice tinged with a thick enough drawl to tug the vowel sounds out like saltwater taffy being stretched.

Louis had found the cabin rental online, then booked it as a surprise. "A camping trip," he'd said, although only Louis would consider an arrangement where they had running water, central air, and electricity as "camping." Gabe recalled the real camping trips they had taken when his dad was still alive, ones with tents, campfires, and toasting marshmallows.

"Why don't you two just go?" Gabe had griped to his mother. "I'll stay with Grandma."

Mom had frowned, but even worse, she'd looked hurt. "Louis thought this would make a great getaway, something we could all do together, a way for us to bond."

I don't want to bond with him, Gabe had thought with a scowl.

The cabin had an eat-in kitchen, the old man said as he unlocked the front door, with two upstairs bedrooms and one on the first floor. He led them on a slow-moving grand tour, with the last stop a large patio in the back. Wooden Adirondack chairs were arranged to face the woods, and beyond it, a firepit had been dug out and lined with cinderblocks.

"You see?" Mom said, nudging Gabe with her elbow when she saw this. "We'll be able to make s'mores."

"Oh, no, ma'am," Mr. Farnsdale said. "Nothing like that. There's a burn ban through this whole area on account of wildfires last year."

"Oh," Mom said, her bright expression faltering. With a weak smile in Gabe's direction, she added, "Well, shoot."

"I'm sure sorry," the old man said.

"It's no big deal," Mom told him, trying to infuse good cheer into her voice. "And anyway, it's such a gorgeous view. Who'd want to spoil it with a bunch of smoke?"

Gabe lugged his suitcase in from the truck, then upstairs to the bedroom he'd picked out. It was Friday afternoon, and Louis had booked the cabin through Monday, which now felt like an eternity away to Gabe. He checked his phone, but they hadn't been able to get much service since entering the mountains, so he wasn't entirely surprised to see he had no reception.

The picture on his home screen was of him as a little boy, still young enough to sit on his father's lap. Dad had been showing him how to thread a sinker onto his fishing line, the corners of his mouth turned up in a soft smile. "One of the few I ever saw from him toward the end," Mom had once told Gabe, her eyes glistening with a sheen of tears.

People asked him about the image, because yeah, it was weird, thirteen years old and having his dad as the background on his phone. Most didn't know what had happened, though, because it's not like Gabe talked about it ever, so he really didn't blame anyone. He'd considered changing the picture a million times but never had the heart. It would feel too much like letting go.

With a sigh, he moved to set the phone aside, put it face-down on the nearby nightstand, out of sight and out of mind, but noticed a notebook that had been left there, with *GUEST LOG* printed on the front. Curious, Gabe picked it up. Inside, he found names and dates in varying handwriting, people who'd rented the cabin before them. Some had also left notes about their experience at the cabin—*Amazing views but wish the water got hotter in the shower!*—or different points of interest they'd visited nearby—*Hiked the Sassafras Trail today. It's marked but the signs are confusing and we wound up going in circles*—or wildlife they'd observed in the area.

The deer here are weird, one entry read, catching Gabe's eye. The author, Hillary R. from Townsend, Delaware, had continued: *They're not afraid of people. You can walk right up to them and they don't run away. They just stand there and watch you. People must feed them, and it's made them tame.*

"You settling in okay?" Mom asked from the doorway.

"Jesus," he exclaimed in surprise. "Don't sneak up like that."

"I wasn't sneaking. I just wanted to make sure you're alright."

She had this way of hovering over him that drove him crazy. It felt like she was afraid to let him out of her sight for more than fifteen minutes at a stretch, because something bad might happen. He knew it was because of his father; Mom had been the one to find him, after all, and blamed herself for what had happened.

"What's that you've got?" she asked, nodding once to indicate the notebook.

"Nothing. A journal I found, something people write in when they stay here."

"That's a fun idea. Maybe we can add to it this weekend."

Yeah, he thought drily, imagining the entry now: *Amazing views, but look out for low-flying helicopter moms.*

"Louis is pretty worn out from all that driving," she said. "Why don't we hang out here for the rest of the day and have an early start tomorrow, get some hiking in before it gets too hot?"

He hitched his shoulder in a shrug. "Sure."

He knew it was stupid, not liking Louis. After all, it had taken years for Mom to start dating again even casually, and Louis was the first really serious boyfriend she'd had since Dad died, the only one she'd liked enough to introduce to Gabe. And he wasn't a bad guy or anything, just kind of a dipshit.

"I'm sorry about the campfire..." Mom began, but he shook his head.

"It's alright."

He remembered Dad helping him skewer a marshmallow on the end of a stick, then hold it just beyond the lick of campfire flames. Had that been the same trip as the one pictured on his phone? It had been so long ago, and he'd been so young, the memories all felt faded to him now, cloudy and indistinct.

"We could try making s'mores in the microwave," Mom suggested now, but Gabe shook his head.

"That's okay."

"Are you sure? I've got the stuff to—"

"It's fine, Mom. But thanks."

She hesitated for a moment, looking uncertain. "Well, come on down whenever you finish unpacking. I brought cold cuts, so we can fix sandwiches for supper."

"I have a great idea." Louis and Mom had each had at least a couple of glasses of wine over dinner, and his voice had taken on a loud, slurred quality. "I saw a bunch of board games on one of the shelves in the living room. Why don't we pick one out and play a few rounds?"

"That sounds like fun," Mom said, adding his empty plate on top of her own.

Gabe, who thought this sounded as much fun as hitting himself in the balls with a hammer, said nothing as he collected the condiment jars from the table and followed her into the kitchen.

"Gabe," Mom said in a sudden, urgent hush as he opened the refrigerator. She stood at the kitchen sink, but her attention lay beyond the window in front of her. "Come quick and look."

She sounded funny, her voice soft and full of wonder, and when he went to stand beside her, following her gaze, he realized why. A large buck and what looked like a pair of either juvenile deer or does had emerged from the forest at the far edge of the yard. They stood motionless in the tall grass, and if it had been any darker out, he might have missed them altogether.

"I can't believe they're so close," Mom said. "Maybe we can get a better look from the deck."

She called for Louis, and Gabe remembered what Hillary R. from Townsend, Delaware had written in the guest log: *The deer here are weird. They just stand there and watch you.*

Through the window above the kitchen sink, he saw that the deer didn't startle at the sound of the patio door rattling in its tracks as Mom pulled it open, or her voice as she called again for Louis, louder now because he'd gone to the other room to get a game.

People must feed them, and it's made them tame.

Gabe followed her outside, and Louis joined them soon after. The three of them stood watching as the deer remained rooted in place, rigid and unmoving, like they'd each been carved from a block of wood, their heads turned in the direction of the cabin.

"Well, there's something you don't get to see in the city, huh?" Louis remarked.

"What do you think they're doing?" Mom asked.

"I don't know," Louis said. "Maybe checking out the fireflies?"

The meadow seemed to have bloomed with hundreds of tiny, flickering pinpoints of yellow light, a winking array that appeared to rise and fall in the darkness like waves on a vast and open sea. It was so picturesque and peaceful that, for a second, Gabe was almost willing to admit that maybe Louis' idea hadn't been so lame after all.

Almost.

The next morning, Mom made pancakes for breakfast.

"I think when you're camping, though, you're supposed to call them flapjacks," Louis joked, and Gabe fought the urge to tell him that no, you weren't, and even if so, this wasn't camping. It was staying in someone else's house, using their stuff, sleeping in their beds, living another person's life—all things that, clearly unlike camping, Louis knew plenty about.

"I thought we could try this loop today," Mom said, unfolding a brochure that included a map of nearby hiking paths. "It looks like there's a trail head not far up the road from here, and it's not super long. Maybe a couple of hours. There's a rest point about halfway, too, with bathroom facilities. We can refill our water bottles there."

Despite it barely being nine o'clock in the morning when they set off, it already felt insufferably muggy outside, the air stagnant and thick. Once they ventured into the woods, the shelter of the trees provided a small but welcome measure of reprieve. Cicadas and bugs buzzed and chirruped in a dense chorus from the tangle of low-lying ferns and flowering plants blanketing the ground. Birds chimed in with disharmonic warbles, flitting back and forth between boughs and limbs overhead.

The trail Mom had picked was little more than a narrow, uneven footpath, and they had to tread carefully as they followed its meandering course. Their progress seemed even slower because because Mom wanted to stop and admire every bush or twig along the way, while Louis kept pausing to take pictures he eventually meant to post on social media. Gabe quickly tired of them both and tromped on ahead.

"I'll meet you guys at the rest area," he grumbled.

"Stay within earshot," Mom called, hovering again, and he flipped a wave to let her know yeah, yeah, whatever.

He'd tucked his father's old compass in one of the pockets of his cargo shorts, and along the way, he paused periodically to pull it out, check his direction. Dad had carried it while stationed in Afghanistan. Gabe had been too young at that time to remember the deployment, but he'd kept the compass nonetheless, if only because it reminded him of his father.

He hadn't gone very far ahead of Mom and Louis, no more than ten minutes, tops, when it occurred to him that the woods had grown quiet, the overlapping whirring and chittering of bugs and birds tapering off. It happened so gradually, at first it escaped Gabe's distracted notice, but now the silence seemed oppressive and strange. Curious, he looked around.

And saw the deer.

It stood no more than ten yards away, hidden among the trees and underbrush. At first, Gabe thought it was a doe, then realized no, he could see two slender shafts of antler protruding from its head, spindly crooks that looked like devil horns. The young buck stared at him, its large eyes black and glossy, its tan and cream-colored coat seamlessly camouflaged against the wooded background.

Gabe first felt surprise, then a breathless sort of wonder, but after a moment in which he stood immobilized with amazement, an uneasy sensation settled in its place, a creeping sort of dread born from the fact that the deer didn't seem to react to him at all. It just stood there, its gaze fixed on Gabe.

What's wrong with it?

The deer stepped out from behind the trees, the leaves beneath it rustling as it lifted its hoof in a high, jerking motion. Another step, another erratic movement, reminding Gabe of the stop-motion puppets in the old Christmas TV special *Rudolph the Red-Nosed Reindeer*, except in real life. With each plodding step, the deer wobbled like a newborn fawn, its movements clumsy, its balance precarious.

What the hell's wrong with it? Gabe thought again. Was it hurt? Or maybe it was sick. Could deer get rabies? He didn't know, but in any case, there was something seriously messed up about the young buck.

Gabe turned, meaning to hurry and rejoin his mom and Louis, but found another deer blocking the trail behind him: a second buck, larger than the first, its antlers longer, wider, bifurcated.

"Uh..." he said, shying back an uncertain step. "Hey there."

As motionless as a piece of statuary, the buck stared at him, its eyes glittering. Maybe it was its proximity—after all, he'd never been that close to a deer before—but it looked much bigger than expected, its legs way too long in proportion to its body, like a circus performer wearing stilts.

"H-hey, boy," he said hesitantly. "Good boy. Are...you hungry?"

The woman, Hillary R., had written in the guest log that she thought people must have been feeding the deer, and it was the only explanation he could come up with for why the two bucks might be acting so strangely bold. He reached for another pocket. Before leaving the cabin earlier, Mom had given him a couple of protein bars to take along.

"You never know what might happen," she'd said.

He'd rolled his eyes because she was helicoptering again, but as he pulled one of the bars out now, fumbling to tear a corner off the wrapper, he felt grateful she'd insisted.

"Here." Pinching off a piece of the granola, he offered it to the buck. "Here, boy."

He added in some *pspsps* sounds because he had no idea how the hell you called to a deer. When it moved, it lifted one of its spindly legs high off the ground just like the first one had. It seemed to have too many joints in places they didn't naturally belong, as if the bones had been broken and splinted haphazardly together again. The effect was eerie, disturbing.

"Here." Not wanting the damn thing to come any closer, wondering again if deer could get rabies, he tossed the chunk of granola. It landed on the ground, but the deer didn't cut it as much as a glance. Instead, it took another of those clumsy, shambling steps forward, then another, its legs buckling and wobbling like a baby learning to walk. He heard a loud rustle from the trees, and turned to find the first buck, the smaller of the two, approaching again, both of them moving in unsteady tandem.

"Okay, you can stop now," he said, throwing another piece of the protein bar at them. Again, they both ignored the offering, their black, doll-like eyes locked onto Gabe.

No, he thought dimly. *Not a doll's eyes—a shark's.*

Only that wasn't right, either, and it took him a moment to realize what it was about the deer—and their heads in particular—that was so unnerving. He'd learned enough in his Earth Science classes to understand the difference between predator and prey. Animals that served primarily as food like sheep, cows, or deer, had eyes oriented toward the sides of their faces, allowing them a nearly panoramic field of vision that helped them better detect danger. An animal that hunted for food, on the other hand, had eyes on the front of their head, like a wolf or dog.

Or a person, Gabe thought as goosebumps rose along his arms and stirred the downy hairs against the nape of his neck. The deer's eyes were wrong, and when he turned to the other, he saw the same: positioned not off-center and to either side of the skull, but instead directly in the front to meet his own gaze evenly.

They have eyes like a person.

"Stop," he said again, this time throwing the entire granola bar, wrapper and all, at the larger buck. It landed with a lackluster smack against the ground. The deer ignored it, hobbling past on crooked, quivering legs, heading straight to Gabe.

"Stop!" With a hoarse cry, he wheeled around and took off, racing up the incline of the trail. Fists balled, arms swinging, feet pounding against the earth, he ran with all his might and didn't dare look behind him. He felt the toe of his sneaker hook an upturned tree root exposed in the path, and fell, landing hard on his belly in the dirt and smacking his chin hard enough to rattle his teeth together. Scrambling to his feet again, he glanced back over his shoulder.

The trail was empty.

His heart pounded, his chest heaving as he gasped for breath, his skin sweat-soaked, his shirt clinging in damp patches to his chest and back. The front of his jeans was now covered in dirt from where he'd faceplanted, and he felt sure if anyone had been close enough by to have caught him on camera, he'd have made the #epicfail Hall of Fame on social media for sure.

I was imagining things. He told himself that was all. Maybe all deer walked that clumsily and strange. *And maybe they all have eyes in the front like that. What the hell do I know about deer anyway? I live in the city. It's not like we have—*

From the woods to his left, he heard the sudden rustle of fallen pine needles, the snap-crackle-*pop!* of twigs and dried pine cones crunching underfoot. From beneath the shadowy overhang of some low-lying tree boughs, he saw a deer—that same godforsaken buck with its devil horns—peering at him.

Oh, Jesus.

At the soft scuffle of cloven hooves through dirt and grit—*trip, trap, trip, trap*—he turned just as the larger buck shambled up the path and into view.

"Go away." He meant to shout this, but his voice came out as little more than a croak as he backpedaled in alarm. "Leave me alone."

The deer continued hobbling toward him, and he bent down, scooping up a handful of loose pebbles from the trail.

"Get out of here," he exclaimed, throwing them at the deer. "I said leave me alone!"

Most of the rocks flew wild and wide, but the few that pelted off the buck on the trail ricocheted without seeming to slow it down or faze it in the slightest. It just kept coming—both of them did—like zombies out of a B-grade horror movie, lurching toward him with silent but menacing intent.

"Mom," Gabe cried. "Mom, help!"

"Mom?" someone echoed—or rather, some*thing*: the deer behind him. With a violent shudder, it suddenly reared back onto its hind legs, towering over him as it stood upright and bipedal, just like a person. It was close enough now for him to see its face had started changing, the fur along its snout wrinkling as its nose receded, as if collapsing into its skull.

"Mom," it bleated, its lips drawing back from the white nubs of its teeth. "Mom, help. Mom, mom, *mooooooooooooooooooom...*"

With a shriek, Gabe turned and ran again. As he neared the crest of the hill, he caught sight of a small cinderblock building: the park service restrooms Mom had pointed out on the brochure map. With a ragged cry, nearly a sob, he ran toward the shelter, all but collapsing against the door to the men's side, pawing desperately at the knob. He threw open the door and rushed inside, shoving it closed behind him. He'd hoped to be able to lock it, and while there was a steel deadbolt embedded for just such a purpose, it was the kind that required a key on either side, which meant it was useless to him.

Desperate, he looked around wildly, then dragged a metal trashcan from near the sinks to block the door. It was a feeble attempt—pathetic, he knew—but it was all he had, all he could think to do. Along the far wall, he saw a pair of urinals, and opposite these, a trio of toilet stalls. Gabe ran to the one furthest from the door, ducking inside and throwing the latch into place. Just as he did, he heard the rattle of the knob from behind him, the sudden clatter as the bathroom door swung open, knocking over the trashcan.

Oh, God, he thought. The panels and door of the bathroom stall didn't extend all the way down, leaving a gap of about two feet of empty space. Knowing all anyone had to do was look beneath the edges to see his feet, he scuttled backwards, then climbed up onto the toilet seat. Pressing his lips together to muffle his breath, he strained to listen.

At first, there was only silence. Then he heard a sound, like a woman walking in high-heeled shoes across the linoleum floor.

Trip, trap, trip, trap

Only Gabe knew this was no woman.

Oh, God, he thought again, wanting to close his eyes, cover his face, hide somehow.

"Mom?" he heard the deer say, a warbling, goat-like bawl.

It's not a deer, he thought, shaking his head, cowering in the corner of the bathroom stall. *I don't know what the hell it is, but that thing is <u>not</u> a deer.*

"Mom?" it said again, and he jumped at the sharp report as the door of one of the neighboring stalls swung open wide, smashing into the wall. A momentary pause, then the *trip, trap, trip, trap* of hooves against the floor again, drawing closer.

His mother and Louis hadn't been too far behind him along the trail. Surely she'd heard him yelling and would be coming to look for him. Surely she'd be there at any moment.

Please, he thought, looking up at the narrow window cut into the wall directly above the commode. It was way too small and too high for him to hope to reach or use it to escape, meaning he was trapped there, completely out of options. *Oh, God, Mom, please, please.*

A hand reached up from beneath the stall door, slender fingers outstretched, hooking against the edge. For a split second, Gabe felt a surge of hope; it was a *human* hand, so maybe it was his mother's and she'd found him after all, had come to his rescue. Then, just beyond the underside of the door, he saw a pair of split black hooves and a head appeared, neck twisted and craning at an unnatural angle to peer into the stall. The deer's black eyes speared into him and he saw its face had changed even more, its ears drooping down, antlers sliding backwards like they protruded from a mound of ice cream left for too long in the sun. Its features looked nearly human now, and hideously—horrifying—it *smiled* at him, a broad leer lined with teeth, its lips stretched wide with glee.

"What...what are you?" Gabe whimpered. "You're not a deer...not..."

"Not deer," it crooned, bending and twisting its forelimbs over the bottom edge of the door, the fur peeling back to reveal bare flesh and those all-too-human hands. Its voice had changed; now it sounded like *him,* not just mimicking his words, but his voice, and with a swell of horror, he realized that's what was happening to its face, too, and its body.

It's changing to look like me!

"Not deer," the creature said again, twisting and writhing as it crawled under the bathroom stall, its gaze black and terrible as it reached for Gabe, who began to shriek. "Not deer, not deer, no, not a deer..."

"Louis, come on," Mom said, appreciating now why Gabe got so aggravated with him at times. After all, he'd stopped yet again along the trail to stare off into the wilderness, even though she'd told him they needed to hurry.

"I didn't hear anything," Louis had protested, but even so, she knew she *had*—Gabe first calling out for her, then minutes later, *screaming.* And even though Louis had tried to reassure her that Gabe was fine—*You worry too much. What could possibly happen in a national park?*—she still wasn't convinced. In fact, she felt the same strange, prickling sort of dread as she had on the day of her husband's suicide, the sense that something was terribly wrong.

"Rachel," Louis said to her now, still standing alongside the trail, pointing toward the surrounding woods. "Look, there's a deer."

Who gives a shit? she felt like snapping, but bit the words back, just like she kept trying to tamp down the melee of fears swirling through her mind—images of Gabe falling and twisting his ankle or breaking his leg; Gabe being bitten by a copperhead or rattlesnake; or mauled by a bear. A million horrifying scenarios, and she kept trying to tell herself she was overthinking, worrying too much, letting her imagination run wild and wooly.

Instead, she kept walking, her pace brisk but not quite running, and within moments, she saw the pitched roof of the rest area as she neared the top of the hill. When she caught sight of her son standing just outside the bathrooms, she uttered a cry of relief.

"Gabe!" she exclaimed, rushing toward him. "Thank goodness! Are you alright?"

He blinked at her, seeming caught off guard.

"I thought I heard you calling for me," she said, feeling foolish now that he was right there in front of her and clearly none the worse for wear. *I thought you were screaming,* she wanted to add but didn't, because he'd roll his eyes or look exasperated if she did, say she was helicoptering again, piloting the ol' parenting Chinook.

He smiled at her. "I'm fine, Mom."

"You sure?" she asked and when he nodded, she laughed weakly. "Well, okay, then I'll make a pitstop since we're here. Louis stopped to look at a deer. Would you mind keeping a lookout so he doesn't wander too far without us?"

"Sure, Mom," Gabe replied.

He continued smiling, and although something about it didn't seem to quite reach his eyes, again she tried to tell herself it was all in her mind.

Louis is right, she thought as she walked toward the bathroom door. *I worry too much.*

DEVILS IN THE DARK

By JG Faherty

NO MATTER HOW hard Eddie Kemper scrubbed, the stench of the beast refused to go away, clinging to his hands like the memories lingered in his head.

The creature spotlighted in his high beams. Brakes squealing as he slammed his foot on the pedal. The acrid smell of burning rubber. The sickening thump of metal striking flesh.

The face... Part monkey, part dog...the long snout filled with dangerous-looking teeth. Pointed ears, like a Doberman's. Deadly claws as long as his fingers. And the eyes...

Even now, two hours later, the thought of those horrible orbs sent shivers through him. Black as night but somehow filled with intelligence and fury as the creature stared up at him, its legs twisted and broken, dark, foamy spit oozing from its mouth. Then the life had faded from them, leaving only a bloody corpse.

And the stink.

It was the worst thing he'd ever smelled, like being in a monkey house in the summer, only all the monkeys were dead and bloated. He'd had to stop and puke twice while lifting the body into his truck – no easy feat, considering it was as big as a damn German shepherd – and then drive with the windows open until he reached the motel.

Eddie rubbed the cheap soap over his flesh again, working up a heavy lather. Although he'd never graduated high school, he had enough smarts to recognize a potential windfall when it landed in his lap. And the dead thing in the back of his '69 El Camino might just be the answer to his dreams of getting filthy rich. He'd done plenty of hunting over the years, but he'd never seen nothin' like the thing he'd hit on Highway 77.

Which meant it could be valuable to the right people.

Which was why as soon as he picked up the two pounds of weed from his cousin Max in Bucksboro, he was heading straight to that big college in Charleston instead of back to North Carolina. There had to be some scientist folks who'd pay major cash for whatever the hell it was he'd found.

Eddie thrust his hands under the hot water.

Now if only he could get rid of the smell...

Max Wayne stared at the monster in the truck and gave a long whistle.

"Dude, when you said you had a problem, I didn't expect nuthin' like this."

You don't know the half of it, Eddie felt like telling his cousin. There'd been nothing *but* problems since he'd hit the damn thing. He'd arrived at Max's house only to find out from Mary-Ellen, Max's dim-witted nag of a wife, that Max was working a double at the Fayette County Fair, repairing generators and wiring the sound stage, *and* he had the weed with him. He'd driven to the carnival, where he'd had to wait two hours before Max took lunch, the whole time imagining the monkey-dog thing swelling up inside its tarp like a dead deer on the highway, getting ready to split open and spill its guts all over.

Then, on top of everything, Max had told him he didn't want to transfer the weed until it got dark, so they'd have to wait until he got off at midnight. Eddie knew the body wouldn't last that long, not with the temperature already creeping toward ninety. Which meant letting Max in on the secret. When he'd lifted the tarp up, the explosion of stink had made them both gag. After tying a handkerchief over his face, Max leaned in for a closer look.

"Damn, cuz...you know what you got there?"

"Nope. It jumped in front of me on the highway last night. Like a freakin' kangaroo. I never had a chance to stop."

"That there's a devil monkey, dude. Didn't think they was real." Max waved his hand and a cloud of flies rose up. "Sure does stink, don't it?"

"Devil monkey? You pullin' my leg?"

"That's what the old-timers call 'em. Every few years someone'll say they seen one. The paper runs a story about boogems and monsters in the woods and everyone has a good laugh. Now you gone and bagged one!"

"Well, I ain't heard of no devil monkey, but I know this thing ain't natural. I'm takin' it up to Charleston to see if one of the colleges will buy it."

"How much you think it's worth?"

Eddie heard the greed in his cousin's voice. There was no getting around splitting the profits, not if he wanted help.

Of course, Max didn't have to know what those profits were...

"A couple of hundred, I figure." Eddie figured it was worth at least three times that. "I gotta keep it fresh, though. I need ice. You help me, I'll give you half."

Max turned to him and smiled.

"Ice? I can do a whole lot better than that."

Eddie sipped his lemonade, relishing the way the sweet-and-sour liquid carved a cold, wet gully through the desert in his throat.

For once, Max had come through for him. The dead monkey-thing was wrapped up nice and tight in its tarp in the snack bar's walk-in freezer, hidden behind racks of frozen burgers, fries, and hot dogs. With the worry of decomposition gone, Eddie was able to relax and enjoy the day, mostly by eating junk and listening to the latest hits by Foreigner and Skynyrd and Queen and Aerosmith blasting out of the fairground speakers. Hearing "Dream On" played at near ear-splitting levels had helped him make another decision.

He was going to take some of the money he made from selling his devil monkey and buy a cassette deck and some kick-ass speakers for the El Camino.

No more eight-tracks for Eddie Kemper.

After downing the last of the lemonade, Eddie checked his watch. Almost five. The demolition derby didn't start 'til eight. After it was over, he and Max would load up the body and he could hit the road. He'd get the weed on the way back home.

As he walked across the fairgrounds to the racetrack, he was already thinking about how to spend the rest of his money.

Behind the wooden platform that served as the concert stage, Max Wayne's walkie-talkie crackled to life.

"Max? We got another gennie that just blew. Where are you?"

Max let out a long, slow exhale, savoring the way the pot smoke burned his throat and tongue. Then he thumbed the talk button on the radio.

"Still at the stage. Ain't nearly done yet."

He'd actually finished checking the amps and lights a half hour ago, but what was the point of busting your butt on a wicked hot night? Let someone else worry about the damn generator. He was finishing his break.

He closed his eyes again and returned to his hazy daydreams of how much money he'd have after Eddie sold that freaky monkey.

It never occurred to him to ask *which* generator had blown.

"Do you smell that?" Evan June sniffed the air, his face wrinkling from the foul odor attacking his nostrils.

"Something's dead," Grady Bach said.

"Yeah." Evan aimed his flashlight at the deep freeze, where one of the fry cooks was just coming out with a box of hamburgers. "I think it's coming from inside the freezer."

Grady shrugged. "Better take a look."

Evan nodded. Looking for a dead animal in a dark room on the hottest night of the summer wasn't high on his list of things he wanted to do. But it appeared they didn't have a choice, not unless they wanted to spend the next hour working in a room that stunk worse than road kill.

Stepping carefully because melting ice had made the metal floor slick as a December sidewalk, Evan worked his way through the freezer, flashlight moving back and forth, sniffing the air as he went.

"It's coming from back here," he said, stepping around a rack full of boxes. A sudden fear rose up in him, the product of too many scary movies where someone stumbled across a dead body.

"Holy Jesus," he whispered. Behind him, Grady echoed his words and added several others.

It was a body on the floor all right, but not human. Evan could tell that just from the two hairy feet sticking out of the rolled-up tarp.

"It smells like it's been dead for a month." Grady waved his hand in front of his face. "I hope that ain't what they're cooking."

"We gotta see what it is." Evan knelt down, using his free hand to tug open the tarp. After a moment, Grady joined him and they unwrapped the body.

"What in the hell...?" Evan's voice trailed off as he stared at the thing. His first thought was someone'd killed a monkey. But a closer look revealed it was no monkey they'd found. Not with those wicked claws and dog-like snout.

Evan reached out toward it.

"What are you doing?" Grady grabbed his wrist.

"I just wanna see if it's real. Maybe someone put it here as a joke." Evan poked it with a finger.

And screamed when its eyes opened.

The creature attacked so quickly Evan had no time to react. He fell backwards, his second cry nothing but a wet choking sound as blood spurted from a jagged slit in his neck and painted the walls and floor.

Grady tried to crawl away but white-hot agony filled his left calf. He rolled over and saw chunks of his leg stuck to the creature's dagger-like claws.

Movement near the door caught his attention and he waved the flashlight at it.

"Help me," he called to the figure, which was only a shadow against the dark night sky. "Please!"

The figure moved closer, stepping into the dim glow of the light. Grady gasped.

It was a twin to the creature on the tarp.

And it wasn't alone.

"Hey, I wonder what all the commotion's about?"

Max motioned with his beer toward a spot in the center of the fairgrounds, where the telltale flashing lights of police cars outshone the neon of the rides and booths.

Eddie turned around. From their seats at the top of the bleachers, they had a perfect view of the fair and the racetrack. He grimaced as he wiped grit from his eyes and caught a whiff of devil monkey. Even though he'd washed a dozen times after he and Max hid the body, the smell refused to go away.

"What's over there?" he asked.

"Yes!" Max pumped his fist as two cars collided in the center of the track. "I dunno. The arcade? Or maybe the snack bar."

A chill ran through Eddie. "The snack bar? You mean, where we hid...you know?"

"Relax, dude." Max chugged some beer. "No one's gonna find our payday. It's hidden behind, like, a thousand burgers."

"So why are the cops there?" Eddie couldn't keep his eyes off the swirling lights. The rumble of super-charged engines and the thundering crash of metal on metal faded into the background as he tried to see why people were running in all directions.

Then he saw them. Shadows leaping and darting among the crowds. Coming closer. Disappearing under the bleachers.

Someone screamed.

Another voice joined the first. Then others.

A second later, all hell broke loose.

"Watch out!" Max shouted, as someone ran into him, knocking the beer from his hand in the process. The pounding of hundreds of feet on the metal bleachers drowned out the growls of sawed-off exhausts. All around them was total chaos, people running in all directions. Some fell and got trampled by the fleeing crowd. Others tumbled down rows of stairs, the sound of their breaking bones lost in the riotous din.

His eyes dull and wide from pot and confusion, Max turned his head back and forth, trying to make sense of what was happening.

Eddie didn't bother. He knew.

They were coming for him.

The relatives of the thing he'd killed. Somehow, its pack had found him, followed him all the way to Bucksboro.

He spotted them as they leapt onto the bleachers like pint-sized kangaroos, a dozen of them at least. Others hopped the barrier fence right into the racetrack. Cars swerved and slid on the hard-packed dirt, smashing each other worse than during the derby itself. That was when Max finally noticed them.

"Holy...Eddie, did you see that? It's...."

Max's voice faded away as he saw the ones climbing the bleachers. The combined reek of the animals hit Eddie like a punch in the stomach and he vomited up his hot dogs and beer. Next to him, Max gagged and put his arm over his face.

From ten feet away, one of them stared straight at Eddie, its black eyes blazing with hatred. It took another step, and the pack behind it followed in unison.

"Screw this!" Max darted to the right, heading for the closest stairs. He made it only three steps before one of the devil monkeys bounded into the air and landed on his back. Max let out a strangled cry that came to an abrupt end when the creature tore his throat out.

Eddie took a step back and the pack moved another step forward. When Eddie tried to step away again, the back of his legs hit the low protective railing that marked the top of the bleachers.

The troop advanced another step.

"I didn't mean it!" Eddie shouted at them. "It was an accident. I'm sorry!"

The lead monkey leaned closer, its lips drawn back to expose over-large teeth. It raised its hands, displaying certain death. The others did the same.

Another step. It was close enough now to touch Eddie without extending its arm all the way. Eddie closed his eyes, not caring that he was crying, not caring that he'd wet his pants, his only thought that he didn't want to die like this.

The barnyard reek filled his nose and coated his tongue. Rough flesh, like the pads of a dog's foot, pressed against his arms and chest. He pictured them all around him, claws ready to tear him to pieces.

His body was in the air before he realized they'd pushed him over the railing. His body tumbled over and then a terrible agony exploded in his legs, accompanied by a *crack* like a tree splitting in a storm. He tried to scream but the pain stole the air from his lungs and all he could do was dig his fingers into the dirt and moan.

How long he lay there, he had no idea. A minute? Five? Time didn't exist, nothing existed, only the pain that grew worse each time he moved. It was the stink of the beasts that made him open his eyes. Their leader stood before him again. Only this time it held something in its arms.

The one he'd hit. Alive.

Even through the red haze of his agony, he recognized it. It glared with the same hatred as the others, its legs hanging broken and useless.

The pack turned as one and bounded away. In seconds, he was alone.

Eddie glanced at himself and saw white bone sticking out of pale flesh.

We're the same, he thought. *For now. But not for long.*

Because no animal could survive those kinds of injuries without medical care. Sooner or later, it would die. And when it did, they'd be back.

It was just a matter of time.

STORM OF THE MILLENNIUM

By Marc Sorondo

EARLIER IN THE day, when the guys on the news had started predicting that what they called a "thousand-year storm" was coming, Jim had assumed they were being dramatic. It had been a slow news week, and reporting on which states had which favorite Halloween candy and where peak foliage would be the coming weekend weren't going to generate much buzz. Alarmist predictions about a storm so intense it only occurred once a millennium, however, would have people talking.

When he'd gotten into his car beneath a sky so obscured by black clouds that he needed his headlights even though it was only mid-afternoon, he mentally conceded that a bad storm was indeed on its way. The shadowed Catskills looked like jagged teeth against that black sky. He hoped he'd make it home before the rain started.

Still though, a thousand year storm seemed ridiculous; they might as well have predicted a dragon attack or a zombie outbreak.

The storm was an enraged beast that filled the heavens and poured its wrath onto the earth. It dumped rain in sheets that made visibility almost nonexistent. The wind blew in gusts that tore saturated foliage from the trees and smacked it against his windshield with a sound that was as sharp and loud as a small caliber gunshot, startling him every time. The deluge struck the car, a perpetual drumroll, and—an instant after every flash of brilliant lightning across the sky—the thunder roared.

The newscasters and meteorologists hadn't exaggerated. As Jim made painfully slow progress down the thankfully empty parkway, he had to admit that he'd never experienced a storm of that ferocity. It was truly a tempest of Biblical proportions.

Normally he wasn't the type to stop for people by the side of the road. He didn't know a thing about cars and wouldn't have been able to help with even something as simple as a flat tire. When he saw the police flashers—distorted by the downpour into a kaleidoscope of red and blue diamonds that danced around the top of the lone cruiser by the side of the road—he felt the bottom drop out of his stomach. As he got closer, he saw that the cruiser was stopped behind a car that had struck a tree head on. The hood of the car was bent up at the middle and the very front of the car had crumpled a bit around the base of the tree, but none of the damage looked as bad as if the driver had been going fast.

The officer on the scene—difficult to make out in the dark and rain—stood beside the banged up car, looking down at the windshield.

That officer was alone.

Jim took a deep breath and pulled over onto the shoulder just beyond the struck tree. He didn't like it, but he felt an obligation to help, at least until paramedics or an ambulance arrived.

The officer headed toward Jim's car as he pushed his door open. The trees, full as they were with leaves that were still just turning and not yet ready to fall, did their best to protect him from the rain but failed despite their efforts. Gusts of wind shook the branches and scattered every drop that the leaves would have held.

"Are you alright?" the officer asked.

Jim was shocked to hear that it was a woman's voice. He'd just assumed it was a man out there in the storm.

"Officer, do you need help? I'm a doctor...well, a podiatrist, but I went to med school. I can help."

"Doesn't matter what kind of doctor you are. Nothing you can do for this poor bastard," the officer said.

"Dead?"

"Dead," she confirmed.

"The accident doesn't seem that bad..."

"I don't think the accident's what did it."

Jim was quiet for a second. "A heart attack?"

The officer motioned to the car and said, "See for yourself if you've got a strong stomach. I'd actually appreciate a doctor's guess as to what happened in there."

Jim nodded and, as he walked past her while heading to the crashed car, he got his first clear look at the officer. She was beautiful in an intimidating way. She had high cheekbones and full lips. She also stood as tall as Jim and had broad, strong shoulders.

"There's a smell in the car." She wrinkled her nose and shook her head. "Never smelled anything like it."

Jim nodded, wondering to himself what good he'd actually be in this situation. He hadn't looked at a dead body since med school. He hadn't examined anything higher than an ankle in well over a decade.

He paused for an instant in front of the car. The center of the hood was crumpled like a sheet of paper that had been held too tight, but only the very front, and he knew that cars were designed to do just that to reduce the force of impact on the driver and passengers. Based on how superficial that damage seemed to him, he guessed that the driver hadn't been going very fast at all when the crash happened.

Then there was the windshield. That was curious. A hole the size of a fully inflated beach ball was cut out of it. An ornate web of cracks radiated outward from the edges of that hole in all directions.

Jim took a few more steps and crouched down to peer into the car through the driver's side window. Between the extreme dark being interspersed with flashes of brilliant lightning and the flow of water streaming over the surface of the window, it took several moments for his eyes to adjust.

The body could have been that of a woman or a slender man. It was impossible to say for sure. The head was gone, the neck just a bloody stump with bits of bone sticking up at the back. The chest was ripped open, exposing the snapped and jagged row of ribs up either side. The abdominal cavity looked to be completely empty aside from a pool of congealing blood at the bottom that splashed when the occasional raindrop was angled just right through the hole in the windshield.

"Officer, I...Officer, what could do this?"

"Do me a favor."

Jim nodded.

She joined him next to the crashed car. "Stop calling me Officer. Call me Bess. Not Beth with a 'th' but Bess with the double 's'."

Jim nodded again. "I will. I'm Jim."

Now Officer Bess nodded, a single, crisp, and efficient movement of her head. "Jim, this morning I would have said nothing could do that. Busting through a car windshield and then tearing a person apart like that...." She shook her head and took a deep breath. She ignored the water that dripped down her face. "Do you have any ideas?"

Jim looked Bess in the eyes. He was close enough to her that even in the dark he could see that her eyes were emerald green. "Shouldn't you call for back-up?" he asked.

"I've requested help several times, but this storm...car accidents, flooding, downed trees. We're spread too thin tonight."

"But this is...well, this is something else."

"Doesn't matter," she said.

A chill ran up Jim's spine. He found himself wondering if, had he not stopped to try and help, he'd have reached his house by now. He wanted nothing more than to change into dry clothes and crawl under a thick blanket.

"You mentioned a smell," Jim said.

Bess cleared her throat. "At first I thought it might be gasoline or some fluid associated with the car. It's not. This is a sharper smell. I almost like the smell of gas, but this sort of burns."

Jim reached out for the handle of the door. "Am I allowed to open it?"

"Technically I should have sent you on your way when you stopped and offered to help. I'll deal with the fallout if there is any."

Jim pulled the handle and then tugged the door open. He expected to have to lean in and sniff inside the car, but even with the gusts of wind and the driving rain, the smell that billowed out of the car irritated his sinuses and brought tears to his eyes. It was an acrid, chemical smell, something like ammonia or nail polish remover but not exactly either of those. He spent a moment ignoring his discomfort, trying to identify the smell. Then he slammed the door and stumbled back a step.

"God, that was awful," he said. Glad for the rain for the first time, he rubbed the cold water into his eyes with the heel of his palms.

Bess grimaced at him. "Did you recognize it? It's a smell I've never smelled before."

Jim blinked at her, rain dripping down his face. "A smell like that would be memorable. You'd recognize it right away." He shook his head. "I've got no idea what it is."

"Damn."

"I'm sorry. I haven't really been much help here."

Bess shrugged. "What about the windshield?"

"The hole?" Jim asked.

"Do you have a sense of how strong a windshield is?"

"Vaguely," Jim said. "Layers of glass and a kind of plastic, right? So it cracks but doesn't shatter."

"Exactly. Not easy to break, but this looks like it's been shot with a cannon."

Jim leaned over to inspect the edge of the hole. The stench that seeped through, even though it was faint, tickled his nostrils. The hole itself was fairly smooth, though a spiderweb pattern of cracks spread out in all directions from it. He thought Bess' description had been spot on: a cannonball going at full speed would tear through a windshield like that, but he couldn't imagine much else that would.

"None of this makes any sense," he said.

"I've been trying to come up with scenarios," she said, "but they all sound ridiculous."

Jim's brow furrowed, but he said nothing. In the momentary pause before she resumed, there was a peal of thunder, a deep note that filled the sky for what seemed an impossibly long time.

"If something strong enough to break through the windshield..."

There was a huge crash, a sound that seemed small and tinny compared to the bass notes of the furious sky.

Jim's car was rocking on its wheels.

Bess pulled her pistol. "Stay behind me," she said. Then she sprinted for the car.

Jim hesitated. He didn't know if she meant that he should follow but stay behind her, or to stay by the crashed car. His curiosity overcame his fear after just an instant, and he ran after her at a top speed that was much slower than hers. He ran into a gust of wind that pushed him back while spraying icy rain so hard it stung his face and slapped him with wet leaves that felt like the cold, limp hands of drowning victims.

Ahead, Bess slid to a stop by the driver's side of Jim's car. There was a flash of lightning that illuminated some amorphous shape within his car.

Bess shot through the window, firing three rounds and shattering the glass between her and that thing in the car.

Jim stopped beside her and looked in at the shape in his car. It was a giant beetle. Its carapace was wet ebony, glossy and reflective and black as a void. It turned to look at them through the now empty window, watching them with multifaceted eyes that looked green, then blue, then a pinkish-purple as a flash of lightning lit them up. It had thick mandibles on either side of its head that it angrily clacked together.

Then the obsidian carapace opened up, uncovering a double layer of gossamer wings that seemed too dainty to possibly lift the gargantuan insect. The wings flapped at such a speed that it was more a vibration than a full movement.

Bess fired one more round as the beetle floated up off the driver's seat.

Jim couldn't avoid the notion that the insect had been counting on his presence in that seat, that he could have been decapitated and gutted just like the corpse in the other car. He watched it rise back through the hole in his windshield, knowing that the thing had been trying to kill him when it smashed itself through that safety glass.

Then Bess was pushing him away from the car and ordering him to run.

The thunder beetle rose over the front of Jim's car, the vibration of its delicate wings holding it at an angle halfway between flat and upright.

"Get to my cruiser," Bess ordered.

This time she stayed with him. Jim ran as fast as he could, his feet sliding in the mud and wet grass, splashing in water that couldn't drain fast enough; she turned twice as she matched his pace to fire back at the beetle as it rose higher and higher over Jim's car.

"Get in the back," Bess ordered. She stopped and turned as Jim reached the door. She fired once and then again as he pulled the door open and slid inside.

The seat was a hard plastic that extended far enough to force his knees against the plexiglass that separated the rear of the car from the front seats. There was a layer of metal mesh over the top half of the plexiglass, another layer of protection for the part of the car that didn't provide a reinforced seat back to protect the officers from the detained.

Bess backed in beside him and slammed the door shut.

For a moment it was quiet aside from their rapid breathing and the machine gun drumming of the hard rain on the cruiser's roof. Then a crack of thunder made them both jump.

After another few beats of relative quiet, Jim said, "Bess?"

"Yeah?"

"Are we locked in back here?"

"We are."

Thunder roared. A bolt of lightning filled the whole sky with white fire for just a flash.

"What are we going to do?" Jim asked.

"If it attacks through the windshield, we've got a layer of plexiglass and a metal partition between it and us. I don't know that it can get up enough speed and force to make it through all three layers."

Jim nodded. "What if it comes at us through the back windshield?"

She sighed. "Then we're both going to die."

There was the sound of the rain and the wind pushing against the car in gusts that made the whole thing rock on its wheels.

"Just to be clear...that thing...it was a gigantic beetle," Jim said.

"It was."

"Maybe it'll go away. You shot it. Several times. You hit it."

"Don't think that did any damage," she said. "The shell is too hard."

Jim thought about the exoskeleton of a regular beetle, and then tried to scale that up. He had no trouble believing that such a covering could be bulletproof.

"Well, then, maybe..."

The sound of the impact was incredible. There was the sound of the crashing itself, the huge thud of that hard, heavy weight striking the glass. There was a sound of shattering as the entire windshield cracked in an instant, but there was also the simultaneous tremendous pop of the plastic layer coming free under the pressure of the beetle, curled up like a living cannonball, blasting through.

The beetle unrolled itself, its mandibles clicking together as it peered through the wire mesh and the plexiglass. Then the mandibles spread wide, the mouth behind them opened, its toothless maw cavernous, and a ball of thick, brown, viscous liquid shot from it and splattered against the partition.

The metal was unaffected, but the plexiglass began to bubble and dissolve immediately, as the acrid stench filled the back of the cruiser.

Between the cacophony of the storm beating on the car, the frequent peals of thunder, the clicking mandibles, and the sound of the beetle's appendages clawing at the metal cage, and the overpowering reek of the creature's digestive juices, Jim was so overwhelmed that he couldn't keep track of all the information flooding his brain. His only clear thought, through all of the literal and metaphorical noise, was that he was going to die, to be ripped open and hollowed out.

Then one of the narrow legs passed through one of the holes in the mesh and reached in where the plexiglass had liquified and dripped away. Bess pulled a set of handcuffs from her belt and snapped one loop closed as tight as it would go around one of the narrow joints that protruded through the metal partition. She hooked the other loop through the mesh itself.

The huge beetle snapped its mandibles and pulled against the restraint.

Jim feared the handcuffs would snap, but there was no leverage or momentum available to the insect. It pulled and pulled, the plexiglass cracking around the oozing hole melted into it.

The carapace opened up and the gossamer wings hummed with motion. The beetle lifted off the seat and pulled against the mesh, which began to creak and pop. Shards of plexiglass rained down on Bess and Jim in the back seat the as the bolts that fashioned the mesh cage of the partition into position bisecting the car snapped off two and three at a time.

When the cage came loose, the weight of it caused the hovering beetle to dip.

Then Bess lifted her pistol and shot it right between the clacking mandibles. The point of impact wept a glossy, black sludge, and the rhythm of the mandibles built to a ferocious speed.

The beetle backed slowly through the hole in the windshield, dragging the panel of metal beneath and behind it, until the cage failed to pass through the hole in the safety glass.

"One more anchor," Bess said as the creature strained against the windshield that kept it from escaping.

Jim turned to find her eyes narrowed and her teeth bared like a snarling, cornered animal.

The sound of the windshield coming out of its housing was almost like a tearing. It was drawn out, as the edges slowly came free rather than the whole thing popping out all at once. The sound had a quality that almost blended into the sound of the deluge but not quite. The windshield, weakened by innumerable cracks, draped over the mesh partition.

The beetle hovered, dragging the combined weight of the mesh and the crumpled windshield backwards down the hood of the cruiser, until it reached the end and dropped out of sight.

Bess made a growling sound and crawled through the opening and into the front of the cruiser. She grabbed a pump action shotgun from a rack that stood between the two front seats, pushed the driver's door open, and got out.

Jim scrambled over into the front and went after her.

The insect was dragging its burden through the mud, making it that much heavier with the material that accumulated on it.

Bess strode in a wide arc until she intercepted the beetle's path. She lifted the shotgun, sighting along the barrel and pressing the butt hard into her shoulder.

Jim thought she was aiming at the carapace, knowing that she'd already tried and failed to crack the armor there. Once she'd fired, however, he realized that her strategy was much more ruthless. Bess was a hunter at heart, and she'd seen a weakness that he, always better at healing than harming, had not.

The shotgun blast passed under the opened carapace and obliterated the delicate gossamer layers underneath. The beetle dropped like a stone and lay atop its muddy encumbrance.

The carapace closed but only partially. What remained of the wings as well as much of the soft tissue beneath was blasted out of shape. As it was, the beetle looked lopsided, with one side's outer covering nearly closed while the other sat at an odd angle.

Bess pumped the shotgun and walked up to the beetle. She held the shotgun in one hand, pressing the barrel into the gap where the creature's armor couldn't quite close.

Thunder roared and Jim saw her, lit from behind by a bolt of whitish-blue lightning that went jaggedly in all directions as it headed from clouds to earth. He would never get that image out of his mind: Bess, her strong body turned and pressing the gun against the monster, lit in profile so that she looked as much like a sword wielding Amazonian as a police officer with a gun.

She pulled the trigger and held the weapon against the recoil that sought to send it flying back out of her grasp.

The titanic bulk slumped down in the mud. One rear leg twitched, but otherwise it had ceased to move.

They pulled up to the station in a cruiser with no windshield, the pouring rain flooding the inside of the car up to their knees. Jim drove so that Bess could ride shotgun, the actual shotgun loaded and pressed to her shoulder as she scanned the sky ahead of them for movement. The station wasn't far from the site of the crash that had brought them together earlier that afternoon, but it still took them nearly a half hour to make it in those terrible conditions.

Jim pulled up in front, killed the ignition, and said, "No one is going to believe us."

"I don't care. Come on." Bess got out, clutching the gun in such a way that Jim thought she might never put it down, and led him inside.

There were decorations in the station—paper vampires, witches, and mummies taped to the doors; several rubber bats hanging from light fixtures in the ceiling, and a plastic jack-o'-lantern on the desk that glowed pale orange. The officer sitting behind that desk, just to the left of the plastic pumpkin, stood when he saw them walk in.

"Bess, what the hell happened?" He came around the desk, taking the turn at the corner so dangerously tight that he barely missed clipping his hip on the corner.

Bess sat in one of the chairs that were arranged in three rows and filled much of the front room of the station. "Have a seat," she said to Jim.

He fell into the chair beside hers.

"Bess, talk to me. What happened to you?"

She hitched a thumb over her shoulder. "This is Jim. He's a doctor. He stopped to help me with an accident, but then we were attacked."

"Oh my god. By who? Are you okay? Did they get away?"

Bess sighed and placed the shotgun on the floor at her feet. "Tell you what, Ryan. Get the tape recorder. I'm not going to want to tell this story twice, and there's going to be a need for a report."

Jim didn't realize he'd been dozing until he woke. It was the entrance of another officer that had roused him.

He'd been loaned grey sweatpants and a blue t-shirt that said APD over the chest in a stern shade of yellow. He'd taken off his saturated shoes and socks, his bare feet cold on the tile floor of the station. He'd been asleep sitting up in one of the chairs, his hands clasped together in his lap and his head lolled forward.

Bess sat beside him in her civilian clothes. She sat straight and tall, her arms crossed over her chest. She had some sort of dark band tattooed around one solid bicep. The bottom half of the ink peeked out beneath the sleeve of a black t-shirt.

Whereas Jim had crashed, falling into dreamless sleep so fast he hadn't felt himself giving in, he knew the instant he looked at her that Bess had been awake the whole time, hyper-vigilant and ready for the glass doors to explode behind her and for another of those beetles to spit foul liquid at her. He would, he expected, have nightmares about the storm and everything that he'd experienced in it for the rest of his life; Bess, he suspected, had it even worse. She'd live those nightmares, ready for them in her dreams and her every waking moment.

The newly arrived officer walked toward them, and Ryan came around from behind the main desk again. The officer exhaled audibly.

"Come on, Davis. What'd you find?" Ryan asked.

"Everything checks out: the car with the mutilated body, up against the tree with a big hole in the windshield; another car with a similar hole and the driver's window shot out. I ran the plates and the first car is registered to a Taylor Davidson, I assume the victim of whatever happened out there, while the second car is registered to a Doctor James Dawson, you," Davis said, pointing at Jim.

"Is Taylor Davidson a man or a woman?" Jim asked.

"If, in fact, the victim is Davidson, she was a woman. Why?"

"Couldn't tell, you know, looking at what was left of her. I couldn't tell if it was a man or a woman," Jim said.

Davis nodded. "I also found a busted up windshield and the mesh partition from a cruiser with handcuffs attached. That last bit was hard to find. Even though the rain is letting up, it was all but totally buried in mud."

Bess cleared her throat. "The bug?"

Davis' mouth puckered. Then he made a small sound of sucking on his teeth. "The other loop of the cuffs was empty. It was latched, but there was nothing in it. No sign of any huge beetle thing," he said. "Unless you count the dead body, destroyed windshields, and the other crazy shit."

"I know what I dealt with," Bess said.

"It's all true," Jim added.

Davis held up both hands. "Hey, hey. I didn't say I don't believe you. Doctor, no offense, but if it was just you telling this crazy story, I'd say you were nuts. I don't know you, and this whole tale is...hard to believe. Now if Bess says she saw something, even something crazy..."

"Then she saw something," Ryan finished.

Davis nodded. "The med guys will do an autopsy on what's left of the body. I'm sure forensics can find all sorts of interesting details about the damage to all three cars. If people don't want to believe you, let them try to make up some story that fits all the details. That's above my pay grade."

ROCK BOTTOM ON LICK CREEK

By Dawn Hilbert

BILL CAME TO live with me sometime in the late nineties. Who can remember the year? The whole decade was shit. One morning my cousin Bree came to my door and pounded away, shouting, "Joe, Joe, where the hell are you?"

I could picture her standing there in cutoffs with a cigarette dangling, her hair in a ponytail like she was still a teenager. I'd already heard the piddly motor of her '85 Datsun as it came down into the bottom and knew who it was before she'd opened her foul mouth. The motor was two octaves higher than the coal trucks that went by up on the hard road.

"What do you want?" I said through the screen door.

"Nice to see you, too," she answered and flicked her cigarette behind her without looking to see where it went. I was in the home place, as we called it, although my great-grandparents who'd owned it had both been dead and buried twenty years or more. It was a low piece of land by Lick Creek, sheltered and cool, where the morning dew was slow to dry. Down in the bottom sunrise was late and sunset early.

She looked around when she came into the front room. "Fixed up the place, have you?"

"Ha ha," I said, not smiling. It looked exactly as it had when I moved in: Mamaw's crocheted afghans layered over the back of the old couch, weird-ass paintings and dozens of Olan Mills portraits on the walls.

"We've got a family problem," she said abruptly.

"No shit," I answered. There was no way to guess which of our assorted surly, discontented family was in trouble. In fact, it would be fair to say if that had been the subject two months ago, yours truly would have been the family member in question. The past six years in Columbus hadn't been good to me. I'd catted around, as my mom put it, been in some uncomfortable situations with some drug dealers I'd had the misfortune to share a house with, gotten two DUI's and a suspended license, and finally lost a good job in commercial construction.

"It's Bill."

"What about him?"

"He's gotta leave his apartment."

Bill was the middle-aged son of—I couldn't immediately remember whose kid he was. He was always at the reunions, seated in the thick of things, with the upright uncles and uptight aunts giving him tight nods and the kids half-afraid of him. It was like he made a hole in the middle of the gatherings, where there was a swirl of people around his perimeter, and hardly anyone breaching that circle of space where he sat.

He was sly, though, and would seat himself at the picnic table where the desserts were, so people had to talk to him sometime, if they wanted the whipped cream and chocolate glop with the crushed pretzels or the blackberry cobbler or the old men's favorite, Beulah's chocolate layer cake.

"What did he do?" He was living down in Madison at a low-income apartment building. He'd had to move when he nearly killed himself here at the home place a few years ago. He'd been pouring gasoline into hornets' nests, and he set the place on fire. That's why the house was empty when I came back to the holler in shame.

"I don't know, exactly," she said. "Nadine sent me to ask you if he can come back here, now there's somebody to keep an eye on him."

Bill was blind. I was a drunk, and I didn't belong here anymore, but I wasn't fit to be in the wider world. That also made me unfit to be a caretaker. Obviously, I had done a shit job of taking care of myself and the little boy me and my ex-girlfriend had made.

"I don't know," I said. "My track record for taking care of people isn't great."

"You can't really say no," she answered, flopping down on the couch and running her hand over the top layer of afghans. "They're cheap yarns, but I always liked these colors," she said. "Mind if I take it?"

She had an eye. It was on top because it was the least garish of them. Mamaw was a penny-pinching farm woman who made real patchwork quilts, all long since claimed by the aunts, and her afghans had dozens of yarn colors in them, as she knit up every foot of every ball.

The one Bree wanted was mostly about three or four colors, with big red circles like polka dots as its main theme.

"Help yourself. This isn't my house," I said.

"Exactly," she said. "Everybody knows you're not staying long. But it'd help us out if you'd take him, while we figure out what to do with him. Maybe we can get him up to Charleston in a different apartment."

"Why'd he get kicked out, again? Did you say?"

She shrugged. Bree catted around, too, but had avoided both marriage and kids. I think she went up to Charleston on the weekends and got it out of her system. How she faced sitting in church every Sunday, I couldn't imagine, listening to the preacher go on about the end of the world coming, over and over every stinking week. It'd made me feel like bring it on, then, so I can get out of this place.

"You lonely here? In the shadow of the movie screen? Bill could keep you company. He's taken up the mouth organ."

"That's probably what got him kicked out of his apartment."

She threw back her head and laughed a big belly laugh, while I looked at her tanned throat and the nice curve of her collarbone that rose out of the neck of her loose t-shirt.

Bill came in about three days later, with Nadine's husband John Wesley and somebody's teenage nephew who carried his boombox, some clothes and personal belongings, and two guitar cases into the first-floor bedroom that I'd cleared out of.

Wes led Bill to the porch and sat him in Papaw's old rocker. I could see a harmonica sticking out of Bill's shirt pocket, and I groaned. Bill didn't look too happy, either.

When he got situated, he said, "Joe?"

"I'm right here, Uncle Bill. Welcome back."

He didn't answer me, and I stood there with nothing to say until Wes and the boy got in their car and drove back out of the bottom. The boy had his window down and thumped the car door rhythmically as they went, although I knew no music was playing in that car.

"Joe, are them holes still there?"

I looked out over the eighteen-inch-tall grass that had taken over what once was a piece of neat yard, fenced with white pickets, half-collapsed and blackened from the fire. I'd mowed one pass around inside the fence line, then said fuck it and let it go.

"I haven't seen any hornets," I answered. In truth, I hardly had been anywhere on the property except the path between the house and my car, which I didn't have a license to drive anymore.

Papaw had sold half of the land when he retired, and they'd built a drive-in theater with a screen that ran along the dividing line. The house sat behind the screen, blocked from the morning sun, but not far enough to block the sounds of people and kids and cars. Their headlights swept across our darkened half of the bottom like searchlights when the film ended.

"Wasn't hornets," he said. He turned his head as if to look at me, but instead I looked at him. His eyes were milky but the old-man skin below them made brown half-moons that held your focus on his eyes.

"Oh. I heard you were pouring gasoline down their nest holes. I don't know I'd risk it, if I couldn't see what I was doing."

He tapped his white-tipped cane. "They're not hornets, though. Go see if you can find any holes."

I cut him a break and did what he asked. I sure hoped he wouldn't try to boss me like this on the regular or we'd have to have it out.

As it turned out, Bill wasn't too much trouble, though he didn't shower enough, and his fleshy lips always caught crumbs and grease smears while he ate. He was a real restless sleeper. And he bugged me every day to look for holes in the yard.

I found a couple and put a thick mixture of dish soap and water into them. I wasn't fucking around with gasoline and catching shit on fire. The holes were big, though. Monster nests. Stubbornly, Bill refused to say what he thought was in them, if not hornets.

Bill spent all day on the porch, and once in a while I'd join him and we'd sit in the old rockers. I didn't have anything else to do, except think of all the things I needed to do and wasn't. Call my sponsor, look for a job, apologize to my ex, make a new start. Instead, I just went on being a dry drunk, puttering, reading back issues of the *National Enquirer* from a tall stack by the couch, sipping sweet tea, and hating myself. It was like the world was spiraling around me, and I couldn't find a place to catch it, something to latch on to and climb back in. Instead, I let it spin around and never did get a good hold on anything.

The night I put the dish soap into the holes, we were sitting on the porch, and I asked him how long he'd been blind. "Since you were born, or did you have some kind of accident?" I asked. It was twilight, and it seemed easier to ask things like that in the dark, when neither of us could see each other.

"It was an accident," he allowed. He shook off a shiver. "Being here brings it back."

I could hear the movie sounds leaking from cars with their windows down. A movement in the grass caught my eye and through the bit of light escaping from the edges of the movie screen I watched a soap bubble rise over the grass.

"Huh," I said. "One of those holes just puffed out a soap bubble."

Bill started like he was sitting on an ant hill. "What'd you say?"

I repeated it. Another, larger bubble broke free of the grass line and rose into the purple.

He bolted out of his chair. "God damn it, they're still here," he said. "I told you to use gasoline."

"Hornets can't breathe when you coat them with soap," I said. "So it's not them. What's causing it, some kind of gas or what?" I laughed. "Papaw should've kept the oil and gas rights."

He didn't answer but aimed his unseeing gaze right at the stream of bubbles that were coming out of the hole now. These were small, like from a kid's bubble wand. I got a sick feeling in my stomach as I remembered laughing as my little boy tried and failed to blow gently through the wand.

Finally, Bill whispered, "Is the spring house still there?"

I didn't have any idea what he was talking about. "What spring house is that, Bill?"

"Go down to the creek and see," he said, louder. "That's where they're coming from. They're tunnelling."

"What the—" I started, and he got insistent.

"Take a lantern and go see if the spring house is standing."

I did know, at the very edge of my memory, where he meant. A shed, tumble-down with gaping holes between the boards, built practically on top of the creek. Mamaw used to keep things in it. And long, long ago, I remember her once sending me with jugs to fill with the icy trickle from the spring. I was probably about six or seven, so Bree was maybe four years old. I remembered her racing up and down the porch steps like a little spitfire and following me on the narrow trail down to the spring house, chattering all the way.

Bill turned toward the house and then back, agitated. It seemed like he was maybe going down into the yard. "You got a gun here?" he asked.

"There's a shotgun in the bedroom, I believe," I answered. "You can't use it, man."

"Take it with you," he rasped.

"What the fuck? What do you think is down there in the spring house?"

"No," he said. "Take the gas can. I think that'll kill them."

I sat there a minute, and bubbles kept rising, drifting up from the grass. It was a little eerie, the bubbles shining with movie light, like we were in our own movie at the back of the other one. I could hear gunfire, so it was a western or a cop film. I could smell popcorn, too.

"Joe."

"All right, all right, damn it."

I went through the house and got out Papaw's big flashlight, but I didn't get the shotgun. I went out the sagging back door and across the sagging back porch, leaving the dusty gas can where it sat by the mower.

The path down to the creek was overgrown with bramble and the flashlight was weak. It was not far, maybe 50 yards. Foxfire glowed here and there. The little drops and cracks of the woods spooked me, but I figured it was Bill's nervousness rubbing off.

My memory was the only thing that hadn't failed me. The spring house was a dark shape in front of the creek, a few steps from the muddy bank. I shone the light over it and heard a slight rustling noise. Finger-width gaps between the boards would let me see in without opening the door, which was ajar but half buried in a mound of leaf mold and dead branches.

Gingerly I stepped close to the side of the spring house and aimed the flashlight into a gap. Some more rustling sounds came, and I saw something shining white down on a plank laid on the ground.

I squinted at it. It looked like some kind of animal nest, with squirming babies in a pile, water rats or piglets or feral cats. They were a mix of white and black.

I stepped back and thought about what to do. Come down here tomorrow and clear it out? No way was I going to burn baby animals alive. I didn't need feral animals running around, though. And I could tell Bill the spring house was gone. I might go up to the house and get a crowbar. There probably was one somewhere on the junk-filled back porch. I put one hand flat on a board and gave it an experimental push, and the whole structure moved under my hand.

When I stepped back and gave it a powerful kick, it collapsed like it'd been made of cards. The dry crackle of ancient boards and whump of the rotten roof instantly silenced the cicadas and the frogs.

Suddenly I felt one of the animals at my feet and sharp claws raking my calf above my unlaced boot. I looked down as something furry encircled my lower leg. I didn't know what it was. It was like a possum or a weasel but about four times as long and with only rudimentary legs. It had wrapped itself twice around my calf and its head was at the back of my leg. Its claws dug into my flesh, and I thought it might have broken the skin.

Adrenalin coursed through me, and I could smell my own sour sweat and the copper scent of blood over the sulfur water in the creek. I needed the thing off me.

I reached down and grabbed it from the side, yanked and threw it away from me. As it splashed into the creek, I saw in the ruin of the spring house another one coming at me. It raised its head and opened its mouth in silent anger. Its face was like a cobra, with half circles of ears standing straight out to either side and fangs gleaming white inside its open mouth. Suddenly it let out a high, scratchy keen.

I didn't know what the fuck it was. Red-eyed, not a mole or snake or weasel or anything else I'd ever seen, and screaming mad. Another, and then two more whipped out from what looked like a hole in the ground, and I ran.

Gasoline it was. I didn't need this shit. Some blood was running down my leg. I looked back once, but the light was so feeble I couldn't see them, if they were following me. They didn't have legs, or much of them, but snakes could move fast.

The old gas can was not on the porch anymore. I shone the flashlight around, but I knew it was gone. I had just walked by it, and it didn't move by itself in the past fifteen minutes.

Around front, Bill stood knee deep in weeds at the edge of the yard, arm extended with the gas can in his hand, splashing gasoline in a wide semi-circle around him.

"Bill, what the fuck." How did he get around to the porch and find that can?

He didn't answer me, and I started toward him, limping now as the scratches on my leg started to sting. I hoped he wasn't carrying a lighter. When I got up close, he started talking.

"We left this place empty too long, I guess. Your mamaw said if you were gonna occupy a piece of land, you needed to be ready to defend it against all other things. I'm gonna run them off. It's still our land."

"Bill, what the hell are they? They're like a snake with fur. Fangs. One wrapped itself around my leg."

He turned his head a little but didn't bother to try to face me. "Don't let 'em bite."

The can was empty, and he threw it behind him and started fumbling in his pocket.

"Get me a light, son."

I protested again, but weakly. I guessed I could get the garden hose if the fire got out of control.

I went into the house, wondering what kind of alcohol might be in there. I told myself it was to clean the bleeding scratches on my leg. I banged through some cabinets over the refrigerator and rooted deep behind the cleaning supplies under the sink. I remembered what Bill had said and thought to myself we didn't own everything. Like the oil and gas rights, we'd given up on what was below the surface.

Outside, Bill cursed in a high-pitched way, and I grabbed a box of kitchen matches.

He was standing in the same place he had been when I left. Something with white fur and black spots was wrapped around his arm. The adrenalin rush came right back and the hair on my neck stood up.

"It's got you! One of them's got you, Bill."

He turned his head when he heard me, then turned all the way around, stiff legged and took a step out of the weeds.

There were five or six of them, squirming, wrapped around his legs up to his thigh. They were making some noise, a hissing, staticky rattle.

Bill wasn't trying to get them off him. Despair was written in the slump of his posture. His arms hung loose at his sides, and his face was a blur with two half-circle shadows below his eyes. While I watched, one came up over his shoulder and struck him a bite on the face.

He went down then, screaming, "I'm already blind, motherfucker!"

I didn't know what to do. If I pried one off, what would the other four or five do to me in the meantime? I thought about pouring gas directly on them, but the can was empty.

I went back to the house and got a garden hoe from the porch, a rusty can of charcoal lighter fluid, and an old buck knife. It was going to hack up Bill's legs some, but it might work to get them off him.

It didn't work. I stabbed at one and it raised its head with its mouth wide and struck at me but missed. After backing up a few feet, I tried the hoe. Bill was lying on his back, his hands around the one who'd struck him in the face and was now wrapped around his neck and head. It had laid itself over his eyes so I couldn't tell if he was conscious or not.

I hooked the hoe between Bill's pant leg and one of the creatures and yanked. Nothing happened. With a more violent pull, I managed to get it free and sling it into the weeds. The next one was too fast and hung on the hoe, crawling lizard-like toward the handle end and I dropped it and stumbled back.

Now I had nothing but the lighter fluid. Maybe fire would scare them. I soaked an old picket and lit it. When I waved it over them nothing much happened, but suddenly the yard was filled with the headlamps of cars beaming around the edges of the screen and the noise of engines. The movie had ended, and people talked and shouted, calling their kids in. Two kids raced around the back of the screen, and I could see their white t-shirts and pale faces staring at the scene behind the scene. They bolted away, whooping and screaming.

It encouraged me, and I started yelling too, trying to look bigger than I was, like there was more than just me, and we were more powerful than them.

Two or three raised their heads and flared their ear flaps just like cobras ready to strike. I grabbed one of Bill's sneakers and dragged his whole body toward me, out of the tall grass. One of the things whipped around and got me on the arm that held my makeshift torch.

I kept pulling, and a couple more released Bill and scurried into the weeds. A voice on the loudspeaker announced the closing of the concession stand in five minutes.

I got Bill's feet up the first step of the porch and left him so I could deal with the one wrapped around my left arm. Its head was in front of me and its red eyes were watching my face. When I stabbed viciously with my knife, it opened its mouth wide and bit hard before falling off me and crawling under the porch.

I called for an ambulance. While I waited on them, I talked loudly and lit a bunch of lights as the drive-in emptied out, and the bottom got dark and quiet. No more of the creatures came toward us, but each one I pried from Bill slithered under the porch.

Bill was alive when the ambulance crew arrived; he even roused himself to croak, "You got to defend your ground," as they loaded him into it.

Boy, did I want to ride with them out of the bottom and into town. Instead, I wrapped a dishtowel around my arm and told them I was fine. I watched them go and made one more phone call before I jogged up the steep driveway, shining the weak flashlight beam behind me every few steps. I sat on a guardrail at the curve right beyond our driveway. All the movie-goers had gone, but the drive-in marquee was still lit. It read "Dogmen" and "Starts at Dusk."

Bree came buzzing up the empty highway about fifteen minutes later. I wasn't sure, but I thought I saw three or four mottled white heads coming out of the undergrowth below the guardrail just as I got into the passenger seat. My vision was blurry, though, and I didn't trust my eyes.

"Do I want to know what happened?" she asked.

"I have no idea what happened," I said. She was turning the Datsun around in the drive-in entrance. "Story of my life, having no clue. If only I'd seen Dogmen instead of whatever I did see."

She snorted a laugh, then cut it off abruptly. "Bill's going to be all right, though, right?"

"He doesn't seem like the type to give up easy."

What I wanted and what I'd planned was for Bree to drop me at the local bar; instead, she did what I asked and took me to a pay phone, where I called my sponsor. I was feeling woozy by then, shook and puny. When I got off the phone, I went over to her side of the car, and she rolled the window down.

"Bree," I said. "I'm not going back there." I handed her the house keys.

She reached out and hooked the keys with one finger. "All right, Joe. I won't argue with you."

"And Bree. If you go back, you're going to need a lot more gasoline."

THE FRIENDLY FROGMAN

By Stephen Bias

"We are always Friendly." The sign mocks me as I drive past it. The adorable irony of it feels like a smug little joke that irritates me every time I see it. There are days God knows why I don't just swerve and take it out with the cruiser's push bar. Folks who live here—and those numbers are dwindling—are proud of that slogan. They trumpet it every chance they get. But I know the truth, and it makes me sick. Residents of this place know to stay indoors after dark. They know better than to go roaming when there's no light. I figure that's why I've been called out of bed at one in the morning. It was one of those instances where someone unaware stumbled upon it, or, in rare cases, a 'Friendlyer' who believes they can tempt fate.

It is a nasty, humid night. The kind that's thick and soupy and chokes you slow. It makes me itch for all kinds of reasons, and before long I'll have a nasty cough that will last me until December. Maybe there's something in the air coming off the Ohio River or the steel plant up the road. Either way, I hate September nights in this town. If I'm being honest, I hate all my evenings here, because eventually I'm going to have one like tonight.

My radio popped to life at that exact moment. It pulled me away from my self-pity about my poor career decisions through the years. It was Riley Henderson, my deputy, and, God, was he a terrible choice. The man was scared of his shadow. He was a living embodiment of Don Knotts from *The Andy Griffith Show*—thin, frail, and utterly useless. He was trying his hardest to sound professional but was failing spectacularly.

"Sheriff, are you close? The woman in the accident is stable. I'm about half a mile up Bens Run Road." A pause. "This is bad, boss... It's... him."

He didn't have to say another word. There would be no other reason to pull me away from the NyQuil-induced coma I was in. Of course it was him. I'd be there in less than three minutes, so I didn't answer. If I had responded, he would have disclosed too much information over the air, and I didn't want to risk the chance of anyone hearing what we were up to.

I arrived on the scene, rolled to a stop, and left the engine running. The moment I slammed the driver-side door, the crickets, momentarily shocked into silence, immediately resumed their raucous activity. For that fleeting second, you could almost pretend it was peaceful. Just another humid West Virginia late night. But peace in this place is just the time you get to take a breath before something stupid happens, and stupid just pulled up in a truck full of bullshit.

In front of me, the whole treeline was having a seizure in strobing red and blue. Riley's cruiser was parked at a crazy angle, its headlights cutting a big, ugly swath into the darkness. His face, when he approached, was already glistening. He always sweated when he was nervous and, combined with the heat, his uniform was so soaked that you could ring it out.

"Spit it out, dumbass," I said. My voice came out flat. I didn't bother putting any life into it.

He just pointed a shaky finger at the mangled heap of what used to be a Subaru. The front end was smashed into a metallic grin, and wrapped up in it was our town's dirty little secret.

Clarence. Just thinking his name made the hairs on my arm stand up. He was sprawled out across the hood like some kind of green, warty roadkill Jesus. Long, webbed fingers curled up at nothing. That wide, stupid mouth of his was hanging open, and his big, oily eyes were staring up at the stars. A little trickle of something like blood, but much thicker, was making a slow crawl from his lips. He was just as disgusting in death as he'd been in life. Maybe even more so.

I stood there for a second, letting the lights paint the whole messed-up scene over and over again on my retinas. Riley was shifting his weight from foot to foot, making the leather of his Sam Browne belt squeak in a way that set my teeth on edge.

"Sheriff," he finally managed, his voice cracking. "What do we do here? What's the protocol?"

I turned to look at him, slowly, so he could see just how much he'd pissed me off. "The protocol, Riley? The protocol is that my ulcer is already acting up, so when we finish, I've got about an hour on the shitter because I stupidly had tacos tonight." I took a step closer. "Next up is the morning, where I'll puke-burp until I've downed a bottle of Pepto, before having to write a three-page report explaining how a state treasure got turned into road pizza by a Subaru. You know what? After that, I think I'll get my ass chewed out by some suit in Charleston who couldn't find this place on a map." My voice was rising now. "What the hell do you think the protocol for a run-over cryptid is?" I let that sink in. "Now, where's the driver, dumbass?"

He lowered his head and jabbed a thumb back at his cruiser. "In the passenger seat, sir. I had her wrapped in a shock blanket. She was pretty shook up. She started doing better right before you showed up."

I nodded. "We're pressed for time. Call Perry to come tow this heap, and for Christ's sake get him off that thing."

I marched over to Riley's patrol car, my stomach twisting into a knot. I could already taste the acid in my throat. It wouldn't be long before I was heaving on the side of the road. I had to remind myself to breathe in through my nose and out of my mouth. I was trying to delay the inevitable for as long as possible. It wasn't helping that I was uncomfortable, my uniform was stuck to me like a second skin, and the only thing swampier than the woodlands off to my left was my ass. My ears were ringing because my blood pressure was skyrocketing. I shouldn't be out here, but there was no one else that could do this. If I'd refused, I would be putting my whole family at risk.

Inside the cruiser, a young woman who couldn't have been more than twenty sat staring at her phone. Her blond hair was pulled back into a tight ponytail. She wore a crimson college shirt from some place with far too many vowels in its name. Her face was pale and streaked with tears, and her eyes were wide and blank. She was smashing at the screen with her index finger as if her life depended on it. What she didn't realize was how accurate her actions truly were.

I didn't feel the need for pleasantries. "You the dipshit that can't drive?"

She shoved the phone toward me; the screen cracked, and the message "call failed" was flashing in the center. "There's no service!" she blurted. "Not a single bar. The GPS led me down this road. My daddy's gonna kill me!"

My gaze drifted from her panicked face back to the wreckage. "I don't care."

Her voice dropped, a disbelieving whisper. "But it was a graduation present."

I kept my back to her, focused on the bigger problem. "Still don't care."

For a long, silent moment, I just stared. Not twenty feet away, a local legend—a thing that had haunted this county for twenty-five years—leaked something that looked like strawberry jam onto the road. He was a hassle, sure, but we were under strict orders to clean up whatever mess he made, no matter what. Even on the night he murdered three teens that were fishing by the river. He was not to be interfered with; just dispose of the bodies and pretend all was hunky-dory. I had wanted to put a bullet in this bastard for so long. It would have been difficult, too. He was cunning and knew this area better than anyone, and somehow he met his end on the front of a Subaru driven by this moron.

"Ma'am." I pinched the bridge of my nose, wondering how I was going to explain all of this to my superiors. "You just ran over a piece of protected folklore. I couldn't give two shits if you get Verizon out here."

She looked away from her phone and off to where Riley was separating Clarence from her Subaru. She clicked her tongue, and the light receded in her eyes. Her lips drew back. She was annoyed, and who could blame her? This was the last place or predicament anyone would want to be in.

"He came out in front of me!" she cried. "I didn't have time to swerve; I didn't have time to do shit! What kind of dumbass runs in front of a car? And what's with the mask? This isn't funny! When my daddy hears—"

"Shut up!" I yelled in her face. She flinched, the phone slipping from her grasp and clattering onto the pavement. My hand shot out, clamping down on her left bicep. There was a moment of surprised resistance, then her mouth opened in a shriek.

"What the hell are you doing! You can't touch me like this! I know my rights! I'll have your badge!"

I knew I was hurting her—my nails bit deep into her skin as I pulled her from the car. She stumbled out, landing hard on her knees before I yanked her back to her feet and began dragging her toward the accident. Her sneakers were scraping against the road as she tried to plant them. Her eyes were torn between anger and fear, but she needed to understand the truth of the situation—and why this was likely her last night on earth.

Riley was still holding Clarence's legs when I hauled her over. The creature was laid out in the high beams, a twisted green parody of a man. I spun the girl around, bent her over at the waist, and shoved her face down toward the corpse. Her screams died in her throat, replaced by an awful, wet clicking sound as she tried to breathe.

"Open your eyes," I snarled, my voice a growl beside her ear. I could smell the faint scent of alcohol on her. She'd been drinking, and if my nose was correct, and it always was, she had a little bit of rum this evening. It was a harsh reminder that I needed a drink myself. "Does that look like a costume to you? You think you could get that on Amazon? This isn't a game. This is Clarence, and you killed him."

She didn't speak, only gasped and let out a low moan. I was about to shove her face right into him when I heard it. A twig snapped up on the wooded embankment to my right. Someone or something was watching. I tossed her to the ground hard and stood rigid.

Please, God, don't let it be who I think it is.

Riley was beside me now, his face pale, beads of sweat dripping off his nose. He held his pistol level at the girl, his arms locked, his knuckles white. He was trembling like someone naked out in the snow. He was panicking, and I didn't blame him one bit.

"Sheriff, just give me the word," he said, his voice broken and on the verge of tears. "Let's hurry so we can get out of here. You know the rules. Just like with those campers—"

I put my hand up. "Put it away, dumbass," I seethed. "You're just going to piss it off."

A shape crashed through the trees and in front of us, oozing out of the darkness and into the lights. He was big, dumb, and clumsy—the B-side to the thing in the road, a younger, doughier model that wobbled with adolescent fat. I'd only seen him once, and from a distance at that. Now I was face-to-face with Mortimer—Morty—the teenage offspring of Clarence.

His eyes were the first thing I noticed—huge, black, and glassy, set so far apart on the sides of his head they seemed to be trying to flee from each other. Stringy, greasy hair, a ghastly shade of green at the root that faded to black near the tips, hung well past his shoulders. It framed a face that was a mess of contradictions: a constellation of slick, warty blemishes dotted his dark green skin, a testament to some unholy puberty. His lower jaw jutted out, a heavy, defiant underbite that gave him a permanent, bulldoggish pout.

His arms were stunted and uselessly short, like a T-rex's, ending in webbed fingers that twitched at his sides. He had an enormous gut that protruded from under his shirt. And speaking of the shirt, Jesus Christ. A faded Nirvana tee, its yellow smiley face stretched into a sick, warped oval. The entire thing was covered in stains that I was certain I didn't want to know the origin of.

He stumbled past me, and I got a nose full of this creature. It was the stink of pond water gone sour, mixed with a deeper rot that clung to things that never see the sun. It was enough to make my eyes sting. It was only then, with him so close, that I realized how damn big he was. He was hunched over, but he still had a few inches on me. I had no idea if he could straighten upright or if he was permanently bent that way. He was thick too, not just with flab, but you could see the muscular lines underneath all that green; he was built solid enough to tear me in half if he had a mind to.

I kept my eyes fixed on the treeline. I didn't need to watch. I knew what was happening. And against my better judgment, a flicker of something ugly and unwelcome—pity—caught me by surprise. I understood what he was feeling. I lost my old man a few months back myself.

That was the moment when he let out a sound of anguish. A shrieking, croaking, bubbling wail that wasn't just noise; it was a physical thing, a wave of the purest pain that vibrated up through the soles of my boots before settling in my chest.

And in the middle of that grotesque opera of sorrow, the woman seized the opportunity. Deputy Dumbass had mentioned killing her right to her face, and let's not forget the fact she was in the presence of a humanoid teenage frog. Her stunned silence was a godsend because I had completely forgotten she was here. I snapped back to reality when, in a sudden burst of movement, she scrambled up and bolted away. She sprinted right past a stunned Riley, across the pavement, and vanished into the muck and mire on the other side.

His grief just switched off, replaced by a white-hot, reptilian fury. He let out a guttural roar and launched forward, hopping after her and away from us both. The whole thing came apart in only five seconds.

I stood there, staring into the empty dark. And there it was. My night officially upgraded from bullshit to a full-blown, category-five clusterfuck. I turned to Riley, who was just standing there, mouth agape, gun still pointing at nothing.

"Couldn't you have stopped her, you useless sack of shit?"

He blinked. A meaningless empty blink. If I didn't have more pressing matters, I'd have grabbed his firearm and pistol-whipped him with it. There was nothing else I could do. I sucked in a lungful of the air that I was certain was poisoning me and set off in their direction.

The woods were a black, tangled mess. The mud was dense, and every stride I took felt as though the earth was trying to swallow me whole. I'd push branches away, only for them to whip back quickly and leave a stinging reminder that I didn't belong out here. I wasn't going to be sneaking up on anyone either; I hadn't realized just how out of shape I was. I could feel my heart beat in my chest, and I was gasping for air already. What was I doing anyway? I should just let Morty have her; it would save me the trouble of dumping the body later. I needed to get Clarence and the Subaru out of sight before morning, and then I could go tell Brenda that her husband was dead.

Brenda. Christ.

The name echoed in my head, like a sour note from a song I hadn't heard in years. She was my date for prom. I recall pinning a corsage to her bony wrist while her father made faces of disgust. He had disapproved of me from day one. I always thought we'd end up together. She was my first everything, but then one night she suddenly vanished from her front porch. For four whole months, the town of Friendly searched for her. Everyone believed that Clarence was responsible for her disappearance. Which he was, just not in the way we'd all thought. How could she end up with...that?

The idea of their biological, physical, and logistical compatibility has kept me awake many a night. How in God's name did that even work? No horror movie could come up with a sequence as horrifying as I assumed Morty's birth had been. Many people at the lodge had wondered out loud how she could bear to do the swamp stomp with Clarence.

I broke through a thicket of thorns and stumbled into a small, moonlit clearing. And there they were.

The woman was stuck. She was sunk up to her knees in thick, black mud, whimpering, her face a mask of terror. Looming over her was Morty. He wasn't touching her, just standing there, his head cocked, a low gurgle rumbling in his chest. To me it sounded like someone trying to speak with a mouthful of water; I had no idea what he was doing. I was unsure whether this was his way of communicating or if the sound was simply natural. But there was something about his eyes, the way he was staring at her, that chilled me to the bone.

"Get away from her! It was an accident. I'll handle this," I bellowed, pulling my pistol. I didn't know if he could understand me. I prayed that he could. I wanted him to back off. I knew a bullet to the back of her head would be quicker than her suffering at the hands of this monstrosity.

Morty turned his gaze in my direction, his huge, gelatinous orbs fixing on me. He flicked his tongue out; it reached well past his waistline, and then he brought it back into his mouth slowly. He was warning me. Telling me not to intervene.

I wasn't going to shoot him, but he didn't need to know that. I stepped forward, and that's when he moved, lunging not at me but toward the girl. I don't know what came over me, but I had to stop him. I dropped my gun and threw myself into him, slamming directly into his doughy middle. It was like hitting a brick wall covered in slime. He tripped over his own two feet, and down we went. I was shocked by how cold he was. His skin was like a sheet of ice. I'd never felt anything like it before. We thrashed around in the mud. "I will take care of her; go home, Morty!" I yelled as his webbed hands engulfed my face.

Just as his strength was beginning to overwhelm me, pushing me downward and deeper into the mud, a woman's voice sliced through the clearing, sharp and commanding.

"Mortimer! You get off of him right now!"

I looked up, wiping the grime from my eyes. A stout figure stood several feet away, holding an old-fashioned lantern. She wore a pink housecoat and wader boots. She looked absolutely ridiculous, but it was her. I hadn't seen her in more than a decade, since I came to tell her Clarence had killed those teenagers by the river. It was Brenda.

She took a step forward; the years had not been kind. Her face was gaunt and covered in moles; her gray hair looked unwashed and was wild in all directions. "What in the hell are you doing, Larry Hicks?" she said, her voice dropping to a dangerous calm. "Get away from my boy."

Morty, responding instantly to his mother, untangled himself from me and shuffled up to her like a scolded child. Brenda's keen eyes scanned the clearing—me covered in mud, the terrified girl, Brenda's agitated son—and then looked past us in the direction of the road.

"Where's Clarence?" she demanded. "Where's that no-good sum bitch?"

"He's dead," I said, making it to my feet. "Back on the road. The girl's car got him."

A long moment of silence passed. A slow, cold smile spread across Brenda's lips. "Well," she said, with satisfaction, "serves him right. He got what was comin' to him."

With that, she paid me no more mind, sloshing through the muck to the girl. "Oh, you poor, sweet thing," she cooed, her voice now oozing with a terrifying, motherly concern. "Just look at you. You've had a terrible fright. Don't you mind Mortimer, baby. He was just protectin' me after his daddy laid hands on me. Trust me, honey, he wouldn't hurt a fly."

She reached down with surprisingly strong hands and pulled the young woman from the mud's grip. The girl, now sobbing uncontrollably, collapsed against her.

"There, there," Brenda soothed, stroking her hair. "What's your name, sugar?"

The sound emerged as a broken wail. "Madison."

"Well, Madison, dear, we're going to get you back to our place. Get you all cleaned up and let you find your bearings." She looked down at Madison, a strange, knowing grin on her lips. "My goodness, this is almost exactly how Mortimer's grandmother found me. Clarence had given me quite a chase, and... well, that's not important right now, sweetheart."

She looked over Madison's shoulder, her eyes finding Morty, who was watching them with rapt attention. Brenda gave him a slow, deliberate wink.

"You just come on home with us now," she whispered to the girl, turning her toward the dark woods. "I won't let that mean old sheriff hurt you. You'll be safe with us."

And just like that, they left. A surreal procession into the dark: the matriarch in her housecoat, an arm wrapped around the dazed victim, and the loyal, warty son lumbering along behind them. I was left alone in the clearing, my boots cemented in mud as I picked up my gun from in front of me.

I had no idea what just happened. What the hell did I just witness? A rescue? An adoption? It was then a nasty thought crossed my mind, and I could feel my stomach drop. I hated this town now more than ever.

Friendly, my ass.

THE ANXIOUS ENTOMOLOGIST

By Damon Nomad

EGBERT CAME UP the stairs of the deck in the early evening. He had a nervous sense that he was late for something as he pulled off his backpack. It was a Saturday during summer break, and he couldn't imagine what he might have forgotten as he opened the glass door to the great room of their new vacation home. An enclave of upscale second homes in western North Carolina, near the highest peaks of the southern Appalachian Mountains.

"Bert! The Rileys have been here for nearly fifteen minutes." Mallory rushed toward him and lowered her voice. "You're filthy. Get a quick shower and change into the clothes I laid out for you. Drinks and snacks in the formal lounge." She whispered in his ear, "Say your apologies for being late. Kayla and Duncan." She knew he had forgotten the names.

He took off his glasses and cleaned them with a soft cloth from his pocket. "I'm so sorry. Time got away from me. I'll be right back." He had forgotten Mallory had invited them, even though she had reminded him several times. He and Mallory were new to the neighborhood.

Egbert found them in the cozy formal lounge after a shower and a change of clothes. He sat next to Mallory. The Rileys were side by side on a matching sofa across from them. A large coffee table filled with assorted finger foods and desserts was between the two couples.

"Sorry again for being late." He remembered that Mallory said the Rileys didn't have kids. Neither did they; he was pleased that there wouldn't be any need for feigned interest in hearing about someone's offspring.

Duncan swirled the drink in his glass before taking a sip. "Mallory said she is a freelance writer for fashion magazines. You're a university professor. What is your field of study?"

"I specialize in Cicadidae." Egbert figured Riley had figured out that Mallory came from a wealthy family. A typical university professor and freelance writer couldn't afford this place.

Mallory winced, "He's an entomologist."

Kayla sipped her margarita. "My mother has hormone problems; she loves her entomologist."

Duncan gently squeezed her forearm. "You're thinking of endocrinologist. Bert studies insects."

Mallory asked, "What about you two?"

Duncan answered, "I'm the managing partner of a brokerage firm. I'm not there that often now; my directors take care of the day-to-day business." He looked at Kayla, "Kayla stays home now. She taught aerobics before we met."

Duncan got up and poured another glass of single malt scotch at the wet bar and sat back down. "Must be nice having the summers off. What were you studying out in the forest today?"

"There is a legend about this area from four to five hundred years ago. Have you heard about it?"

Kayla and Duncan looked at each other and quietly shook their heads.

Egbert continued, "A clan of around one hundred Cherokee lived in these foothills from spring to late autumn. They were a part of a large tribe further south in the Piedmont. They came here to forage, plant some crops, and hunt until winter started to take hold in the mountains." Egbert spoke in a quieter voice "One year, they never made it back south. None of them."

Egbert leaned forward. "The tribe sent a scouting party the next spring, and they found their lodges were still standing. They were filled with skeletons, and the skeletons of their horses were outside. No sign of being attacked by enemy tribes. The bones were picked clean of any flesh."

Kayla gasped. "Wild animals killed them?" She moved closer to Duncan.

Egbert answered, "Not according to the tale. There were drawings on the ground in several of the lodges of a large insect."

Kayla's eyes went wide open. "They were eaten by bugs?"

Egbert shook his head. "No, it's just a myth. Folklore that had been passed down from generation to generation. A French explorer documented it in his journal in the early 1800s. The ancestors of the tribe told him the story and replicated the drawings. His book has a sketch of the insect that is based on what they drew for him. It looks a bit like an oversized locust."

Egbert waved a finger in the air. "Fables tend to have some element of truth. I have a theory of what might be behind this legend. Locusts can be terrible pests. Might have destroyed their foodstuffs, and maybe they weren't able to leave. Many of them could have died during a harsh winter. Possibly an extinct subspecies."

He shrugged, "I have a copy of the explorer's journal. There's a rough map, but it's hard to match it to the modern terrain. I was looking for any sign of where the lodges might have been. I didn't find anything, but I only covered a few acres."

Kayla shivered. "I never much thought about this forest having wild animals. Bears and wolves creeping around outside our home."

Duncan kissed Kayla on the cheek, "There are no wolves or bears in these woods. Right, Bert?"

"Definitely no wolves, but there are surely bears." He frowned, "Thousands of acres of protected national forests are nearby. Lots of coyotes, foxes, weasels, poisonous snakes, and some hawks." He mumbled, "Nature is full of killers."

Mallory shook her head. "Kayla, there's nothing out there to worry about. Bert always frets about something lurking in the shadows. Poisonous frogs, spiders, and even plants."

Weeks later, Egbert scribbled notes in his field journal at a spot deep in the forest. He pulled off his backpack, got out his water bottle, and took a drink. He put his field journal and the water bottle back into the pack and pulled it over his shoulders. He was excited about the survey results from his recent trips into the forest. It would take nearly an hour to get home, scrambling over the rocky and hilly terrain. He could make it back before it got dark.

Egbert reached into his pants pocket and pulled out the handheld GPS. He eyeballed the route the device was pointing toward. He remembered scrambling over the large boulders nearly two hundred yards away. He muttered to himself, "That's the right way." His thoughts were on his strange findings from the past month as he headed toward the rocky outcrop.

He heard the excited screech of a barn owl as he scrambled atop a massive rock. He instinctively turned toward the sound and saw the blur of a large bird coming right at his face. He lost his balance and fell backward off the big stone. Egbert hit the ground hard, and it nearly knocked the wind out of him.

He sat up, took in a deep breath, and exhaled slowly. He could tell he hadn't broken any bones, and he wasn't concussed. Luckily, he landed in a soft patch without stones or large rocks. He spotted his glasses on the ground next to him; they also made it through without any damage. He rubbed them clean and slipped them on.

He mumbled as he stood up, "Could have been worse." He was positive that he heard the screech of an adult owl and thought he caught a glimpse of something chasing it as he fell. Something big enough to chase a barn owl? He wondered.

He felt a bead of sweat coming down his forehead. There was blood on his fingers when he wiped it away. He used some gauze from his backpack to gently rub the spot. There wasn't much blood on the thin white bandaging. He held the gauze on the spot for a few minutes, and there was no fresh blood. Just a scratch from one of those tree limbs.

He pulled out the GPS and checked for the next landmark on his route. It was the crest of a hill about a thirty-minute walk away; he recognized the spot. There was a well-worn footpath between the top of the hill and the edge of the garden at the back of their house. He took a drink of water and ambled off toward the hill.

He wondered about what he had seen and heard. Hawks were known to hunt owls if prey was scarce, but this forest was full of small critters, much easier to hunt than a large owl. He was sure that something flying had been chasing the barn owl. Had to have been a hawk. It was the only thing big enough. His mind went back to the peculiar and interesting results in his journal as he headed home.

The next evening, Egbert finished getting dressed in the master bedroom. "Not that shirt. It clashes." Mallory shuffled toward him with a dark gray designer shirt in her hand. It looked pretty much like what he had on, but he never argued with Mallory about what he should wear.

He quickly changed shirts and raised his hands with palms facing up. "Okay?"

Mallory's eyes studied him up and down. "You're a handsome man when you get cleaned up with a proper shave and run a comb through that hair. Wish you would think about contacts instead of those glasses." She ran a finger near the scratch. "You're lucky that tree branch didn't hit you in the eye."

She shuffled back a few steps. "We need to get going; remember, the Dolans and Rouseaus will be there. Drinks and heavy hors d'oeuvres."

He slipped on his sports coat. "I'm ready."

It was only a ten-minute drive to the Rileys' home. He had met both the Rouseaus and Dolans before; all four were nearly seventy. The women had never worked, and both had faces that seemed locked into perpetual smiles from Botox and plastic surgery.

Arthur Rouseau was the former managing editor of a large newspaper and fancied himself an intrepid investigative journalist. Clarence Dolan was a retired attorney and litigator who represented corporations and their senior officials in business matters. Dolan had political connections and liked to name-drop important people he associated with.

Duncan Riley greeted them at the door. "Right on time." He gestured to the great room.

Everyone was seated in easy chairs that had been arranged in a circle with a large circular cocktail table in the middle. It was covered with finger food, beverages, silverware, and dinnerware. Egbert settled into a seat next to Mallory with Duncan on the other side of him.

Duncan waved a hand at Egbert. "What happened, Bert? That looks like a pretty nasty scratch."

Egbert shrugged, "An encounter with an owl and a hawk in the woods." He paused, "It must have been a hawk."

Kayla pulled her lips off her margarita glass. "My God. You were attacked by a hawk. That forest is dangerous."

Mallory waved her hands. "Bert! Don't exaggerate. He fell off a boulder when an owl screeched at him. He was scratched by a tree branch."

Clarence Dolan chuckled and took a swig of his bourbon. "Spooked by an owl, professor?"

Egbert poured himself a drink as he began his explanation. He took a sip of the G&T as he finished up, "Must have been a hawk."

Duncan finished off a few shrimp cocktails and wiped his hands with a napkin. "What is it you've been so focused on out there the past few weeks? Looking for those Cherokee lodges?"

"No, something more peculiar. At least from a scientific perspective. I've been surveying some of the species to study the food chain." He spoke in a hushed voice, "Some unidentified creatures are competing with the natural predators."

Arthur Rouseau snorted, "What are you saying? That some unknown creatures are living in the forest?" He sneered, "You're supposed to be a scientist. Not a fearmonger talking about monsters."

Egbert's eyes narrowed as his lips curled into a frown. "I didn't say monster. I can show you the expected ratios of known reptiles, amphibians, birds, and mammals that are known to live in this ecosystem. I've studied several dozen acres near the center of the forest. Some other predator is out there, and it has disturbed the food chain. Something big enough to take down a weasel or a fox, and it moves fast. Possibly hunting in a group."

Kayla gasped, "A pack of wolves?"

Egbert took a swig of his drink. "There are no wolves. But I haven't been able to identify what it is."

Arthur Rouseau pointed a finger at Egbert, "Why hasn't someone seen something unusual out there? Lots of people hike in this forest."

"I think it's just shown up in the last few weeks. It hasn't always been here. But they are now. Whatever it is."

Kayla slurped her margarita. "A fox. My cat is not as big as a fox. I let her join me on the patio sometimes. Is she in danger?"

Egbert gestured with a gentle wave. "I wouldn't worry if you're there with the cat." He paused, "But if I had a cat or a dog, I wouldn't let them wander free near the edges of the forest."

Ginna Dolan's eyes widened. "I was talking to Darlene Strickland yesterday. She said their little terrier just disappeared a few days ago."

Clarence Dolan growled, "A missing dog. Don't get hysterical. Probably just wandered off into the forest."

He gestured at Egbert. "Don't go spreading rumors. You make it sound like man-eating tigers are on the loose out there. You study bugs, not apex predators. Don't send people into a panic."

Egbert felt Mallory squeeze his thigh under the table. He bit his lower lip. "You're right. There's no reason for people to be worried." He paused for several moments. "But something is out there. Something not in the textbooks for this region."

Arthur Rouseau chuckled, "Like a killer owl."

A few days later, Egbert was checking the bird feeders on the edge of the garden in the back of the house. He saw something lying in the mulch. He bent down and picked it up. It looked both peculiar and familiar. What did this come from?

Egbert spent several days studying fragments under a microscope and reviewing references in the home study and on his computer. He express mailed a piece back to the university to get a colleague's opinion and a DNA sequence.

In the late evening, nearly a week later, his mobile phone buzzed as he worked on the computer in the small study. He tapped on the phone, "Hi Stanley, you got something on this specimen?"

"It's quite interesting. I agree with your speculation about what it seems to be, but I have never seen anything quite like it. I haven't been able to match anything in the databases."

"Same for me working here. Anything yet on the DNA?"

"Just got it a little while ago, and I took a quick look. Frankly, I don't know what I'm looking at. I just emailed the file to you. You have more depth in that area than me. This could be an exciting discovery. I've kept it a secret like you asked."

Egbert clicked on the email icon. "Okay, I have the email and the attachment. Let me take a look." He clicked the mobile phone off and opened the file with the DNA sequence.

He lost track of time as he worked to unravel the mysterious genetic sequence. He did not hear Mallory come into the study. "Bert, have you been up all night? You never came to bed."

Egbert turned his attention away from the computer monitor. "Yeah. Sorry. What time is it?"

"Nearly eight-thirty in the morning."

He jumped up, grabbed his backpack in the corner, and bolted past Mallory. "I'm going to the forest."

She shouted, "The Rileys and Dolans are coming here for dinner at six." She chased after him, "This is our first dinner party. Back here, showered and dressed by five. I'm not kidding."

Egbert stumbled as he came up the stairs onto the deck. He nearly fell to the floor as he threw the door to the great room open.

Mallory shouted, "Bert, what's going on? You're a mess. Our guests have been here for nearly twenty minutes."

He bent over with his hands on his knees, trying to catch his breath. "I ran." He panted loudly, "I ran most of the way back."

He stayed bent over until he got his wind back. The Rileys, Dolans, and Mallory were staring at him like he was a madman as he stood up.

Duncan Riley shuffled a few steps toward Egbert. "What's going on, Bert? You look a bit out of sorts."

"I've been searching all day. I finally found what's out in the woods, and I know what it is. We need to get somewhere safe."

"We're safe. What do you think you found?" Clarence Dolan sipped his drink as he stared at Egbert.

"This room isn't safe. Somewhere without windows." He paused, "We should go to the cellar."

Mallory crossed her arms on her chest. "What are you ranting about? We aren't going to the cellar. The catering company just left; the dinner is in warming pans in the kitchen."

Egbert moved back to the glass door that opened onto the deck and looked outside for a few moments. He moved away from the door to the wet bar and poured himself a gin and tonic.

He took a long drink, then took in a deep breath and slowly exhaled. "I found something unusual in the garden nearly a week ago. I sent a piece to a colleague and had a DNA sequence done. It looked like a fragment of a wing from an unknown locust species."

Dolan snorted, "You want to hide from some bugs."

"It's not a bug!" Egbert lowered his voice as he took off his glasses and cleaned them with a soft cloth. "It's not what we would think of as an insect. The DNA is from something ancient: the time of dinosaurs."

He put his glasses back on as he continued, "A cross between a cicada, a locust, and some sort of carnivorous arthropod. I think the eggs stay dormant deep in the ground for five hundred years or so. Then, they burrow out of the ground as nymphs, similar to a cicada. The nymphs climb up into a tree, where they mature. When they're fully developed, they go on a feeding spree in swarms like locusts. They're omnivores. They will eat whatever fruit, plant, or meat they can find."

Dolan shook his head. "Sounds like science fiction and wild speculation. You're letting your imagination and nervous disposition cloud your judgment."

Egbert finished his drink and put the glass on the coffee table. "I saw them, thousands of them, in the forest up on large branches in the trees. Some of them have matured and are moving about. They are nearly a foot long, and they look like giant locusts. They're all getting ready to take flight. This must be the same thing that killed the Indian clan here five hundred years ago."

He waved his hands. "We need to get to the cellar." He raised his voice, "Right now!"

Mallory put her hands on her hips. "Have another drink, take a shower, and we will all sit down for dinner."

Clarence Dolan poured another drink. "Yes, get a grip. What makes you think they would attack people or any animal, for that matter? They are just big bugs."

Ginna Dolan looked out the glass door leading to the deck. "You have such a beautiful garden." She nearly shouted. "Oh my! Is that Darlene Strickland running through your backyard?"

Egbert ran to the door, followed by Mallory, Kayla, Duncan, and Clarence. Egbert opened the door and shouted, "Darlene. Are you okay?" There was a loud buzzing sound coming from the trees in the forest.

Darlene stopped and turned toward them, screaming, "Help me!"

Moments later, several giant, buzzing, brownish-green insects knocked Darlene to the ground. The creatures began to rip at her flesh with their leg burrs and chattering mouths. She managed to stand and stagger a few steps toward the deck. Her clothes were tattered and blood-soaked as she tried to pull one of the small monsters off her head. She fell back to the ground and disappeared under a blanket of the creatures.

Ginna Dolan slumped against her husband. "They're killing her."

Clarence sighed, "There's nothing we can do."

Egbert gestured toward the trees. "There's more of them." He slammed the door shut. "Quick, to the cellar." A swarm, hundreds or thousands, of the flying monsters poured out of the forest. Moments later, everyone heard the creatures slamming into windows all around the house.

Everyone followed Egbert as he bolted down the hallway. They heard windows breaking as they ran through the narrow corridor. The buzzing sound grew louder as the creatures poured into the house.

Egbert shouted, "It's right here."

Duncan yelled out as he trailed behind, "Quickly, they're behind us."

Egbert slammed the cellar door shut just as Duncan came inside. Moments later, they heard the thumps of the bugs hitting the thick wooden door. Egbert found the switch that turned on the bare bulb hanging from the ceiling.

The sounds of the little monsters slamming into the door grew louder, and there was a grinding sort of gnawing sound. Duncan asked, "Egbert, they can't eat through wood. Can they?"

Egbert was quiet for several moments. "Oh my. Maybe the cellar wasn't the best choice."

RIBBIT

By Christopher Markman

STEVE WAS SWEATING a lot. His brother had talked him into a week on the Appalachian Trail. They'd started at the southernmost point, in Springer, Georgia. It was the second week of July, which Steve thought was frankly a stupid time of year to walk the trail. The good news was that the altitude and shade combined with frequent breaks made it tolerable. They had gone only a few miles when Jon decided to leave the trail and head north through the thick brush. Steve, who had come along at his mother's admonition to keep his brother out of trouble, was not amused.

"Jon, what are we doing?"

"Enjoying nature, bro!"

"I was enjoying it on the trail."

"Too many people. Scares away the animals. This is nature at its purest."

Steve slapped another mosquito, well, slapped at it. The damn thing flew to freedom, hovered, and looked for a new avenue of attack. Steve saw a relatively clear piece of ground, walked over, and sat down. "Dude, we're lost."

"Nope, GPS!" said Jon, holding up the little device.

"Do you even know how to use that?"

"Yeah, I took a course from the outdoor store!" Jon always talked in a way that you could hear exclamation marks. The guy had one mode, perpetual excitement.

Steve looked at his phone. He wanted to check a couple of things. He waved his phone at his brother. "Dude, no signal. Suppose we need help?"

Jon pulled out another little device. "I give you the PLB or Personal Locator Beacon. If I set it off, the signal goes by satellite, and the Air Force will come get us."

"Uh huh." The mosquito made its decision and came in. It was a distraction, and one of its buddies flew into Steve's ear. "Gahhh!" said Steve, sticking a finger deep into his ear. The original mosquito went for the jugular. Jon dropped a mosquito net hat on Steve's head.

"Never say I don't look out for my older brother!"

"Dude, this is insane. We need to head back to the trail."

"Mañana, mi hermano. It's getting late. We need to set up camp for the night."

The brothers got up early. Without the distraction of the internet on their phones, they had fallen asleep at sunset. After breakfast, the men shouldered their packs, and Jon said, "This way."

"I may not have your GPS doohickey, but I know we came from that way." Steve pointed back behind them.

"Yeah, but this way lies a hundred thousand dollars!"

Oh man, thought Steve to himself. *Jon's on another treasure hunt.* Ever since they were boys, Jon had been after one treasure or another. "What now?" asked Steve, resigned.

"The Cryptid Foundation will award 100K to anyone who finds Squirrely frogs! There are legends going back to the Native Americans of small tree frogs that eat squirrels. We're almost to the middle of their habitat."

"The frogs are not what's squirrely."

"Come on, dude! I've got a theory! You know how much people like to exaggerate. I figure these little critters eat mice or something. James Ogelthorpe wrote about them in his journal, and so did Andrew Ellicott. You know I always do my research! Little guys are about the length of a grown man's thumb. They look like regular tree frogs except their feet aren't webbed, and they have actual claws! And teeth! Lots of little shark-like teeth!"

Steve dropped his pack and sat down.

"Aw, don't be like that!" whined Jon.

"Do you have a plan?"

"Well, duh!" Jon reached into his pack and pulled out a small wire cage. Inside were six mice. "I brought bait! We'll set this up along with cameras and some sticky pads. With luck, we'll catch one or more of them. Then we'll be famous. We'll have finally found and proven that Squirrely frogs do exist!"

"Dude, if they do exist, can we name them something better than Squirrely frogs?"

"If we find them, you can name them," said Jon magnanimously. "But only if it's something cool. I get a veto until you get it right." That had been one of their games as boys, a sneaky way of making sure the other brother did it your way.

"Whatever," said Steve.

Several hours later, there was a beep. "We're here! This is where old Ellicott said he saw them!" said Jon.

"Great. Time for a rest." Steve tossed down his pack. The brothers spent the remainder of the day looking for tree frogs, but couldn't find any. As the sun began to set, they found a good spot to set up camp.

"I bet the frogs only come out at night!" exclaimed Jon. Later, after they'd pitched the tent and eaten, a croaking sound began. "Dude, it's them!" Jon, eyes huge with excitement, dug the mice and some GoPros out of his pack. He set them up and then retreated to the campfire.

Chirping frogs were around them all night, but in the early light of dawn, the mice were still in their cages, untouched.

Steve didn't say much. He just glared at Jon while waiting for the water to boil so he could have coffee and breakfast. Jon ran from tree to tree, trying to find one of the frogs, but with no success.

The sun came up over the mountains about the time breakfast was finished. The frogs had grown silent. It was as if they were never there. Steve stayed in camp. He bathed in a nearby stream and took it easy after two days of hard, sweaty hiking. This was supposed to be a vacation. He should have known it would be one of his brother's harebrained stunts. So, while his brother ran around in the woods, Steve read and took a nap.

That evening, the chirping was even louder. It was so loud that Steve had trouble falling asleep. At home, he lived near an airbase. Loud, very loud planes came and went at all hours. Steve had even slept through tornado warning sirens. So, these frogs were loud. It didn't help that Jon went charging into the brush with a flashlight. Eventually, Steve fell asleep to a cacophony of frogs and the cursing of his brother.

Steve woke as the sun began to lighten the horizon. His brother sat by the burning embers of the campfire, dejected. Jon's shoes were off, and a couple of toes on each foot were taped.

"Broken?" asked Steve.

"Don't know. Really sore. I can barely walk. Left foot hit a big ole root and the right hit a rock. We'll have to start back today. We'll be lucky to make it back to the car before we run out of food." That was a surprisingly rational and adult thing to say for Jon.

"I don't want to run out of vacation either," said Steve. "I like my job and my boss. Steve put some water in the pot. When the water was hot, he made instant coffee and a dehydrated breakfast skillet.

Steve ate while Jon stared moodily at his captive mice. "Maybe you used the wrong bait," Steve said. Jon looked up. Steve tossed a bit of reconstituted bacon into the cage. "Everything's better with bacon."

Jon sighed with frustration at his brother's attempt at humor. Then, a frog landed on the cage and flowed through the wire bars. Its tongue flicked out and grabbed the bacon. "More!" whispered Jon excitedly. Steve tossed another piece, but it fell short of the cage. The frog hopped to the edge of the cage and his tongue extended out, but it was unable to reach the bacon. Another frog landed next to the piece of bacon and snapped it up. The sound of the frogs, which had become much quieter overnight, began to increase.

Jon jumped up and hobbled over to his pack. He pulled out his own breakfast skillet and added water. He only gave it a minute and then began saying "ouch, ouch, ouch," as his fingers dug through the hot package looking for the bacon. He started throwing the bacon in a wide arc, and more frogs appeared.

Several times, a bit of potato or pepper came out with the bacon. Each time, the veggie was ignored, and only the bacon was eaten. After the bacon was gone, Jon pulled out beef stroganoff. That met with a hearty froggy approval as well. Jon went digging into his pack for another meal.

"Better not," said Steve. "You're already going to be hungry by the time we make it back."

"Yeah, you're right. I got video, though. I GOT VIDEO!" Jon sang.

"That doesn't prove much. You need a frog." They turned and looked at the mouse cage. It held five mice and one very fat frog.

"Mission accomplished," said Jon. Then he looked at the frog. "And I shall name you Primo."

Jon limped slowly along. Every species name that Steve came up with, Jon vetoed. By the end of the day, they were only one-third of the way back to the trail. They were going even slower than Steve had feared. He had Jon put his feet up and take some aspirin for the pain and swelling. Steve set up the tent, got water, and performed all the other little chores to make camp. Mostly, they used a propane stove to heat water, so they didn't need wood. Steve was too tired to collect wood and build a fire anyway.

As the last of the light faded, the brothers took a close look at Primo. He or she did indeed have claws, but they were rather dainty. They looked good for climbing, but not for hunting prey. Neither brother could get it to open its mouth.

As soon as Steve fell asleep, Primo started croaking. *Loud little guy,* Steve thought. Then he rolled over to go back to sleep. Primo was joined by another, then another. Soon, the noise was loud enough to hurt Steve's ears. He and Jon could communicate only by yelling or hand signals. Jon grabbed a flashlight and climbed out of the tent. He turned the light on, and thousands of little eyes reflected the light. Jon turned slowly in a circle. They were surrounded by a sea of frogs. Frogs hopped from the back to the front. The circle of frogs was constricting.

"Get back in!" yelled Steve. As soon as Jon was inside, Steve zipped up the tent. They were safe. Then Steve felt foolish. Tree frogs. Tiny little tree frogs had intimidated them into hiding. Still, he didn't feel like going out to confront the amphibians. And, apparently, neither did Jon. They both lay down and pretended to sleep.

Steve woke up. He didn't know what time he fell asleep, but now the sun was well up. It was also quiet. The tent was getting hot and stuffy. He woke Jon. Then, they carefully unzipped the tent and looked out. Not a frog to be seen.

Their phones said it was 10:30 a.m. They had lost hours of hiking in the light. They quickly packed and resumed their trek. They could eat trail mix. Just before they started walking, Jon said, "Hey, look at this!"

Steve looked, and Jon held up the mouse cage. Now there were two fat frogs and four mice.

"Primo's got a girlfriend! We'll name her Sally!"

Steve looked and saw there was some difference between the two frogs. The smaller one had a darker throat. Did that mean boy and girl or just a random difference? And which one was Primo? Steve decided he didn't care. He was tired from lack of sleep and frustrated from their slow pace. They needed to get on the trail.

Both brothers collapsed. They seemed way more tired by the slow pace than they had been by the earlier, faster pace. Fortunately, they would reach the main trail tomorrow. Steve again had Jon take it easy. Maybe his toes were better, or maybe not. At least they weren't worse.

"Hey, look at this!" called out Jon. Steve looked, frustrated. Jon had started digging through the leaves and held up a deer skull.

"Yeah, deer skull," said Steve sarcastically.

"Yo, this one is fresh. The whole skeleton is here."

"We've found them before, dipwad."

"Not like this. All the bones are here. Nothing's scattered. Coyotes or buzzards always scatter the bones. This looks like an anatomy table or something."

"Great," said Steve, not really paying attention.

The sun was just barely below the horizon when the frogs started singing. The nights before had started with one lone frog, but tonight the little froggy symphony started from the first croak. If anything, the frogs were noisier than the night before. The brothers, by silent but mutual consent, retreated to their tent. Inside one of the frogs in the cage was singing as well. One frog inside was hardly a match for the hundreds that were outside.

Neither brother was able to fall asleep, so Steve was not awakened by Jon's scream. The side of the tent was dimpling. It was like hail hitting the side of the tent. Steve thought it was the frogs, but he wasn't going to open the tent and look out. The pummeling continued all night.

Dawn did not bring a cessation to the froggy escapades. Only when the bright light of the sun hit did the noise die down and the frog storm stop. After half an hour, Steve stuck his head out of the tent. The frogs were gone, and the brothers left ten minutes later. The cage now held two frogs but only one mouse.

The brothers reached the main trail at seven p.m. Both were exhausted from the trek, lack of sleep, and the fact that they hadn't taken the time to eat. They hadn't stopped to filter water either, so they didn't have enough to cook with. At least setting up camp hadn't taken long.

Jon had wanted to push on, even in the dark. However, he'd reinjured the toes on his left foot, and this time they were swelling pretty badly. "If I'm not better in the morning, I'll call for help," said Jon.

That evening, they were zipped into the tent before the sun finished setting. However, the night was quiet, and they quickly fell asleep. Jon looked in his cage. He had two fat frogs and zero mice.

Steve awoke to a scratching noise. He looked around. Jon was snoring softly. Steve figured what he had heard was Jon's snoring when the sound was repeated, and then several more times. Steve grabbed a flashlight and turned it on.

Jon was awakened by the light. Steve held a finger to his lips for silence. The sound had stopped when the light was turned on. After a couple of minutes, Steve decided he had been hearing things. "Sorry," he said. He turned out the light and lay back down. He wiggled around to get comfortable and was just nodding off when the sound resumed. He sat up and turned on the light.

Jon, far from looking annoyed, said, "I heard the noise too. What is it?"

Steve shrugged, and the brothers sat waiting. Both were exhausted. After a bit, Steve attached the light to a loop in the top of the tent and lay down. If whatever it was didn't like light, he'd leave the flashlight on. Both brothers fell asleep.

Steve woke to the noise again. The battery in the light had run out. "Jon," he called out.

"Yeah?" came a sleepy voice.

"The batteries ran out on my light. Turn on yours." Jon did so and was rewarded with the sight of frogs in the tent. The sides had numerous cuts, and frogs were crawling through them into the tent. "Gaah!" Jon yelled.

"Sush!" said Steve. The inside of the tent was covered with the little frogs. Some of the frogs had their mouths open, showing sharp teeth.

"Piranha frogs," said Steve. "That's what we should name them."

"Good name, bro!"

The brothers were not missed for several more days, well past when their phone batteries had run out of charge. It is little appreciated how hard it is to find lost hikers. Normally, searchers start from the PLS or Point Last Seen. For the brothers, that had been the parking lot at the trailhead.

Searchers don't search for people; they search for clues. Dozens of untrained people will turn out to help with a search. In this case, a volunteer found a cage with two cute frogs. It did not strike him that this could be associated with the lost hikers. Being a bit of a frogophile, he decided to take them home.

THE HIDDEN WILDS

Created by Michael Fitzgerald

THE HIDDEN WILDS is a solo journaling RPG. You'll create your persona for the session, learn about the cryptid you're searching for and, using a deck of playing cards, a wooden block tower (Jenga style) and a notebook, will chronicle your adventures.

How To Play

The turn is simple. You'll draw a card and review a chart. You'll next journal the scene. Then you'll draw one (or more) cubes from the tower. You'll visit locations, experience events and have encounters. Along the way, if the tower ever collapses, the session comes to its conclusion.

When drawing cards, you'll match the value to one of the charts to get the selection. If that value has already been pulled for that chart, ignore the pull, lay that card over the previous matching card and pull the number of cubes from the tower as cards now in that pile. (i.e., if the number 3 card was previously pulled for Location, and this was the second number 3 pulled for a location, place it on top of the first and pull 2 cubes from the tower).

When you choose your subject from a chart to journal, the color of the card dictates whether the event goes favorably for you, or the location is more hospitable towards you. If you encounter someone, how they react should be determined by the color of the card. Black is favorable, useful or gainful, while red is unfavorable, dangerous or possibly hostile.

For example, a backpack found during a black card event might have lost notes in it, while a backpack with a red card event might have a snake!

Setup

Shuffle a deck of cards and set up a stacking tower. Grab a notebook or a few sheets of paper and something to write with. Some mood music often helps. Draw a card and consult the Persona chart. This is who you are for this adventure. Write a brief bio about this person and why you are out investigating today.

Now, draw a card and consult the Cryptid chart. Use the suit to choose its origin and the rank to choose its form. This is the nature of the creature you'll be investigating. Make a few notes about what you've heard about it. It doesn't have to be a complete description; you'll learn more as you go along. Let's start your adventure.

Each turn comprises (3) Actions, each followed by journaling your experience and pulling cubes from the tower. You will move to a new Location, have an Event, and search for a Clue. You will continue these turns until you locate the cryptid (the tower falls).

Turns
> (Move) Draw a card and consult the Location chart.
> Create a journal entry
> Draw a Block(s)
> (Event) Draw a card and consult the Event chart.
> Create a journal entry
> Draw a Block(s)
> (Investigate) Draw a card and consult the Clue chart
> Create a journal entry based on the adjective selected.
> Draw a Block(s)

Pulling Blocks from the Tower

When you create a journal entry, pull a block from the tower and add it to the top. Remember, if the card pulled has already been played, you will pull additional cubes from the tower!

Concluding the Session

If the tower falls, you have an encounter with the cryptid, and it's time to journal the session conclusion. Fully describe the cryptid. Was it curious, was it angry? Describe your emotions, from the fear of coming face to face with the beast to the thrill of finally discovering/learning the truth.

You've now written your own tale of cryptid adventure.

Tips

Here's some advice to help you chronicle your adventure.

- Don't panic if the scene doesn't come to you at first.
- Keep it simple. Just describe where you are and what you see.

It always helps if you mention how you feel about what's happening to you at the moment. Are you at ease in the location or do you have the sense that you are being watched? Talk about the weather, the smells, the sounds.

If you are stuck, you can think about:

- What's out of place?
- What am I not being told?
- What happened here?

Charts begin on the next page.

The Charts:

The Persona Chart

Card Drawn	Persona
A	Lost – Break Down
2-3	Journalist
4-5	Podcaster - Cryptids
6-7	Park Ranger
8-9	Author
10-J	Searching for Lost Person
Q-K	Land Owner - History

The Cryptid Chart

Card Drawn	Cryptid (Origin / Form)	Description
♠	Folkloric	Ancient tales, part of the local culture
♥	Cosmic	Something alien to this world
♣	Scientific	A bio-experiment gone wrong
♦	Spirit / Curse	A tragic death, cursed lands
2-4	Animalistic	In the shape of a known animal
5-7	Humanoid	Upright, could be mistaken for a person
8-10	Shifting	A mass or cloud. Hard to contain
Face	Intelligent	Might communicate, has a goal
Ace	Unknown	The accounts always differ

The Location Chart

Card Drawn	Location
A	Woods
2	Creek
3	Cabin
4	Mine Entrance
5	Rocky Ledge - Overlook
6	Farm
7	Shrine / Rustic Altar
8	Cemetery
9	Archaeological Site
10	Old Church
J	Field
Q	Makeshift Shelter
K	Worn Path

The Event Chart

Card Drawn	Event
A	Find an item
2	Animal Call
3	Hurt yourself – basic
4	Light rain
5	Encounter*
6	Find a backpack
7	Sound of branches breaking
8	Something running through woods
9	Sense of foreboding
10	Smell of smoke
J	Encounter*
Q	Encounter*
K	Think you see the cryptid

* Draw a new card and consult Encounter table

The Clue Chart

Card Drawn	Clues
A	misty
2	hollow
3	wild
4	ancient
5	prickly
6	delicate
7	rusted
8	grimy
9	new
10	strange
J	foreign
Q	burnt
K	scarred

The Encounter Chart

Card Drawn	Encounter
A	Ranger
2	Campers
3	Hikers
4	Fellow Investigator
5	Police
6	Hunter
7	Herbalist foraging
8	Students – study group
9	Strange person
10	Injured Person
J	Artist
Q	Possible Government Agents
K	Friend – Surprise Encounter

Example Session

Drew an 8♠ for the Persona - Author

Journal entry:

I'm Walter Floyd. I write local-interest stories for the town paper. Between holidays, the story choices get slim, from choosing seeds for your garden to getting rid of kitchen pests. Today I left the house for a break and went on a small adventure to explore the sightings of a regional cryptid. I hoped that might pull a few new readers to the dying periodical.

Drew a 8♣ for the cryptid – Shifting / Scientific

What I've heard was there was a WWII lab that made explosives hidden in the backwoods. There used to be a stream of workers bussed in daily. Inside that lab were secret experiments that created a creature with no form, or an unstable form that could move through small openings. During an accidental explosion that damaged a portion of the lab, it managed to escape.

Now we begin!

Drew a 10♠ for Location – Old Church – favorable

I parked in the lot of Our Savior of the Spirit Church, a worn old-school church with a rotted steeple and open front doors; ready to welcome visitors. This church had become a focal point for sightings and disturbances over the years. They believed the entity was a more spiritual occurrence than supernatural or manmade.

Note: since it was a favorable card, I had the doors open in the church.

Pulled a cube.

Drew a 5♥ for Event – Encounter – pulled another card & consulted the Encounter chart

Drew a J♦ for Encounter – Artist – unfavorable

Sitting alone on a pew was an older woman with a large sketchbook. She was facing the front of the church and did not notice me enter the building. She was sketching

wildly in what appeared to be charcoal. I couldn't tell what she was drawing from where I stood. On the pulpit were a simple lectern, a few wooden chairs and a large cross made from old lumber with iron nails holding it together.

As I walked up the aisle, she shut the cover on the sketchbook and stood, clutching it to her chest.

Pulled a cube.

Drew a 8♥ for Clue – Grimy – unfavorable

I noticed her hands were covered in charcoal. The cover of the sketchbook was completely smudged. I told her my name and tried to engage her in conversation about the church and her drawing, but she backed away from me. I stopped, not wanting to press my luck with her.

Pulled a cube.
Etc.

CONTRIBUTORS

CECIL ADKINS lives in Huntington, WV, with his wife Tiffany, who is also an author. When he isn't (barely) surviving his retail management career, he writes science fiction, romance, and urban fantasy under multiple pen names, always seeking the balance between the strange and the deeply human.

From his home in Barboursville, West Virginia, **STEPHEN BIAS** spends his days making up stories and his nights writing them down. A connoisseur of the absurd and a student of local legends, he blends unfiltered rural horror with a cynical, humorous voice that could only come from the Mountain State. He is the author of the novels *304 Monsters* and *Afterwords* and is currently writing a handbook that details the protocols law enforcement should use for dealing with cryptids run over by motor vehicles.

JD BYRNE was born and raised around Charleston, West Virginia, before spending seven years in Morgantown getting degrees in history and law from West Virginia University. He's practiced law for nearly 25 years, writing briefs where he has to stick to real facts and real law. In his fiction, he gets to make up the facts, take or leave the law, and let his imagination run wild. He's the author of eight novels and numerous short stories exploring weird and fantastical themes. He lives outside Charleston with his wife and the two cutest Chihuahuas the world has ever seen.

Born and raised in New York's haunted Hudson Valley and more recently a resident of North Carolina's equally haunted Cape Fear region, **JG FAHERTY** is the author of 25 books, four collections, and more than 100 short stories, and he's been a finalist for both the Bram Stoker Award (twice) and ITW Thriller Award. He writes adult and YA horror, science fiction, dark fantasy, and paranormal romance, and his works range from quiet, suspenseful horror to action-packed paranormal thrillers. He is proud to be a relative of Mary Shelley. You can follow him on X, Facebook, and Instagram as @jgfaherty.

MICHAEL FITZGERALD is an award-winning playwright and filmmaker. His short stories have been published in several anthologies. He worked with Dawn Hilbert selecting the stories. In his spare time he plays tenor saxophone in a community band.

DAWN HILBERT is a writer, reader, and bookseller at Cicada Books & Coffee in Huntington, WV. She helped select the stories in this collection. Although she is at work on a Gothic historical novel, she also had a cryptid story to tell.

S.E. HOWARD grew up in the heart of Kentucky, the Bluegrass state, and has worked as a newspaper reporter, travel writer, and magazine editor. Her horror short story, "You've Been Saved" was adapted for film in the 2022 independently produced anthology *Worst Laid Plans* by GenreBlast Films. Other horror titles include the novella *Prairie Madness* with Baynam Books Press, and her novel-length debut, *The Vessel,* with Wicked House Publishing. Find out more at www.sehoward.com and www.facebook.com/sehoward.author.

REBECKA JARRELL grew up in the small town of Talcott, WV and now resides in Huntington, WV after graduating from Marshall University. A lifelong reader and collector of hobbies, she has a specific love for quirky, heartfelt stories for middle grade readers.

BEAU LAKE is a tattooed and blue-haired horror and romance writer skulking around the mountains of Virginia. She is very happily married and lives with a menagerie of children (3), dogs (3), and plants. Her current hobbies include digital art, social/animal activism, and screaming into the void. Mostly the latter. Other favorite activities include listening to true crime podcasts, staring at empty Word documents while having existential crises, and asking herself "What Would Stephen King Do?" Some of her published work includes: the DC Pride series, co-written with Tatum West; the paranormal romance series The Wolves of Wharton; and the upcoming horror series Allgood. She can be found online via Facebook, Twitter, or at beaulakebooks.com. She loves talking with readers and can be reached at authorbeaulake@gmail.com.

CHRISTOPHER MARKMAN is a former Naval Submarine Officer and corporate drone. He now raises grass-fed organic lamb and beef on a small farm in rural Alabama. He's been a member of a Search and Rescue Team covering North Georgia. He started writing stories at his daughter's encouragement.

DAMON NOMAD is the pen name for an author who writes short stories, essays, and novels. You can find a collection of his short stories and essays on Writing.com. Commercially published work includes two novels, *Phantom in the Desert* and *A Dangerous Test*, both published by Speaking Volumes. He has short stories published in several anthologies and journals, including *Jane Nightshade's Serial Encounters*, *Arithmophobia: An Anthology of Mathematical Horror*, *Suburban Nightmares*, *Inanimate Things Volume Two*, and A *Twist in Time*. He is a member of the International Thriller Writers Honorary Society.

B. B. NOTT was born and raised in Appalachia. She's been writing since she was old enough to pick up a pen and has a love for all things horror. She currently lives with her two cats, who she's pretty sure aren't secretly cryptids. Probably.

ZACHARY SMITH spent the majority of his adult life in Asia and Africa working in education, environmental research, energy, and disaster management. Born in Huntington, WV, he splits his time between Singapore and the KYOVA Tri-State area, where he teaches, writes speculative fiction, and tries to garden, if not performing daddy duties or sword fighting at Renaissance Faires.

MARC SORONDO lives with his wife and children in New York. He loves to read, and his interests range from fiction to comic books, physics to history, oceanography to cryptozoology, and just about everything in between. He's a perpetual student and occasional teacher. For more information, go to MarcSorondo.com.

Born in 1992 in Orlando, Florida, **MAX TACKETT** moved to Kentucky when he was seven and spent his early childhood fascinated with all things weird and scary. His first experience with nightmares came from a Batman poster hanging up in his room when he was a child. Enlisting in the Marine Corps in 2011, Max continues to utilize his traumatic experiences to illustrate vile and tasteless horror experiences.

www.ingramcontent.com/pod-product-compliance
Lightning Source LLC
Chambersburg PA
CBHW061919130726
47908CB00017B/2298